The Ghost of Gilman

A Calvin York Mystery

By

Rod Beach

The Ghost of Gilman

Rod Beach

This book is a work of fiction. The events and characters described herein are imaginary and are not intended to refer to living persons. The opinions, descriptions, and characters described in this book are solely the opinions and words o of the author, except when they were presented with reference to specific data on the internet.

RBA Publishers
6747 S. Dover Cir.
Littleton, CO 80128

rbanda@comcast.net

PRINTED IN THE UNITED STATES OF AMERICA

The Ghost of Gilman

Other Books by Rod Beach

Calvin York Mysteries

Triple Play
Middle of Nowhere
Sanctioned
Missing Penny
Smoke on the Mountain
Unlikely Abduction
Fourteen Days of Havoc
Kokapelli Killer
Deadly Politics
The Chase to Murder
Nowhere to Run
River of Death
Butte Force
Tragedy in Tin Cup

Other Books by Rod Beach

Dirt Dogs
Dusty Sandals
Wet Feet in Seal Skin Boots
Peace and Harmony in New Chaco

The Ghost of Gilman

Dedication

This book is dedicated to all my old friends and family who guided me not only in my early days but also during my later years on this earth. Particularly, Norm who has encourage me in my writing, helped me numerous times with my computer, and even helping me proof this story.

Thank you, Norm.

The Ghost of Gilman

Prolog

When I start a new book in this Calvin York Mystery series, I search the different data bases for unusual places within my adopted state of Colorado. In this book, I came across the most recent Ghost Town in the state called Gilman. There are numerous posts from people who broke the law and went into Gilman to take pictures of this place with such a rich history.

As one post by 'Legends of America', provided me with the history of Gilman. Sitting on the side of Battle Mountain about 12 miles southeast of Avon, Colorado is the old company town of Gilman. The now abandoned town was originally founded in 1886 by miners searching for silver, but later became a center of lead and zinc mining.

By 1876 several lode silver-lead deposits had been found in the area, setting off the Colorado Silver Boom. The rush began in nearby Leadville, as thousands flocked to the town to dig for their fortunes. Soon, the miners spread out, with many of them filtering down Tennessee Pass, traveling over old Ute Indian trails. As more adventurers swarmed to the area, the trail was widened to allow teams of mules or oxen. However, the route remained treacherous and was aptly named "Battle" for a reason.

By 1879, ore strikes were made in what would become the Battle Mountain District, the first in Red Cliff. The same year, Kelly's Toll Road opened, generally following the same path as present-day Highway 24. It started in Leadville and continued over Tennessee Pass and down Battle Mountain to the Eagle River Valley. Numerous miners then spread deeper throughout the canyon and on to the steep slopes of Battle Mountain.

Judge D.D. Belden discovered what would become the Belden Mine in May 1879. Later that year, Joseph Burnell, a Leadville newspaperman, discovered what would be developed into the Iron Mask Mine. Other mines would soon be discovered including the Black Iron, Ida May, Little Duke, Ground Hog, May Queen, Kingfisher, Little Chief, Crown Point, and Little Ollie, the oldest dating back to 1878.

Here, a number of mining camps sprouted up called Belden, Rock Creek, Bells Camp, Cleveland, and Clinton (later called Gilman). By 1880, Battle Mountain had a smelter, a stamp mill, a sawmill, and a mining district with elected officers to settle disputes about the scores of scattered mining claims.

The Denver and Rio Grande Railway reached Redcliff in November 1881 and by the next year extended through Eagle River Canyon with a station at Belden at the base of Battle Mountain. By this time Redcliff had become Battle Mountain's first boomtown, with two saloons, several hotels, an opera house, and a number of other businesses.

One of the many area miners during this time was a man named John Clinton, who was also a judge and speculator from Red Cliff. In the early 1880s, he acquired a number of mining operations in the vicinity, including the profitable Iron Mask Mine, which would become the principal producer of lead and zinc within Colorado for decades.

Near the Iron Mask Mine was a growing population of log cabins and tents along the steep mountainside. Clinton soon improved the mining operations and established a mining camp on a 600-foot cliff above the Eagle River on a flank of Battle Mountain. Sitting at an elevation of 8950-feet, the camp was named for him. The first building in

The Ghost of Gilman

Clinton was a saloon built in 1884.

In 1886, the Iron Mask Mine constructed the first tramway on the slope of Battle Mountain to connect the mine with the railroad at the bottom of Eagle Canyon. Afterward, the mine began shipping over 100 tons of ore per day. The same year, the Colorado state inspector of mines estimated that the Iron Mask contained 100,000 tons of ore worth $3,482,000, and the mine's workforce of fewer than 80 employees doubled in two weeks.

With the increase in mine production and the bright prospects for the future, the Clinton mining camp quickly transformed into Battle Mountain's second boomtown. In 1886, it received its first post office and was renamed Gilman to avoid the chance of confusion with Clinton, California. It was named for Henry Gilman, the well-liked superintendent of the Iron Mask Mine. Henry Gilman had also donated land for a schoolhouse and served as president of the first school board.

By late 1887, the fledgling town boasted a hotel, a boarding house, a general store, a billiard hall, a sampling room, a newspaper called the Gilman Enterprise, several saloons, and a population upwards of 1,000 people. Like many other mining camps, it also hosted a number of rowdies who might ride their horses into a saloon, shoot out the lights, and conduct acts of banditry and violence.

By 1890 the initial rush was over, and the population of Gilman dropped to 442. The silver crash of 1893 caused an immediate cessation of many of the mines and the Battle Mountain mines decreased production. The operations at Gilman would not resume fully for twenty years.

In 1899, Gilman was almost entirely destroyed by a fire that took down the Iron Mask Hotel, the school, the shaft house of the Little Bell Mine, and much of the business district.

By 1900, some $8 million in silver, gold, and lead ore had been recovered on Battle Mountain. However, by this time, the area mines were no longer producing much silver and turned to mining zinc.

In 1905, The Eagle Milling and Mining Company reopened the Iron Mask Mine with a new emphasis on zinc production and installed a roaster and magnetic separator that separated out the zinc minerals. In 1912, the New Jersey Zinc Company began buying up the claims and land on Battle Mountain, including the town of Gilman, and the days of independent miners came to an end.

The Iron Mask Mine was renamed "Eagle 1" and "Eagle 2" by 1919. The mining operations transitioned increasingly to zinc, although the Eagle Mine was still the leading producer of silver in the state in 1930. Eventually, the mine boasted 62 miles of tunnels beneath the mountain.

I would encourage the reader to look at the various posts on the digital data of pictures of this town and the people who made their living in this dangerous place.

Although this mystery is a work of fiction, many of the elements of the town and the nearby towns of Red Cliff and Minturn are featured as well as Eagle County, Colorado. A visit to these places is highly recommended, not only for the beauty of the area but for the history that remains.

Chapter 1

It was a cold snowy day in Denver in the middle of January as I got ready to go to work. Looking out the kitchen window, I noticed there was at least six inches of snow on the road in front of our house., I decided to take my time getting into work. I knew most of the Colorado Bureau of Investigation Offices would probably be empty this morning, but I had promised my boss, Sidney Kingsbury, I would look over Detective Johnson's notes to see I could find a clue that would help him solve his current case.

Mary, my wife, decided to keep the nine-year-old twins, Hector and Sally, home from school and they were playing with my three-year-old son, JR, when I left for work. As I went out the door, Mary asked, "Are you sure you need to go to work today?"

"Yes, I told Sidney I would help Detective Johnson this morning since he wants to make an arrest tomorrow. I plan on coming home as soon as I complete that task," I said as I left the house.

The roads through Lakewood were covered with snow and snow plows were out removing snow and those where to the side of the main roadways. It took me more than an hour to drive just twelve miles. There was a small fender bender at one major intersection, and I helped one old lady push her car away from the curb.

When I pulled into my parking space, I noticed only three other cars sitting there. I noticed one of them was my Secretary Joyce's car. When I walked into my office, I saw Joyce sitting with another woman in my chairs in front of my desk. Joyce looked up and said, "Cal, this is a friend of mine. Her name is Joan Ault and she is worried about her parents. She hasn't heard from them for over a week and they usually call her at least every other day. She has also tried to call them three or four times and no one answers the phone. She called me last night since she knew I worked for the CBI and I thought she should talk with you. She only lives three houses from me, so she just came in with me this morning."

I looked at a woman that looked to be in her upper forties but still very attractive. "Joan, tell me what concerns you," I said as I sat down at my desk.

Joyce got up and asked, "Cal can I get you a cup of coffee. It is ready now, so I was going to get Joan and me some."

"Yes Joyce, you know I need my coffee," I responded as I took out my notebook to jot some notes down as Joan told me her story.

Joan sat in her chair ringing her hands and finally said, "My father and mother lives in Red Cliff, Colorado. He is a retired miner at the Gilman Mine. Mom and Dad always calls either me or my brother Albert Wise at least every two days but neither of us has heard from them for over a week. I am worried that something may have happened to them."

"I see," I said. "I need to determine what county Red Cliff is in. I will call the Sheriff and have him go to their home to have one of his deputies check on them. What is their address?"

"They bought an old house at 872 Water Street back when the mine closed down. The United Mine Workers received a large payment from the Government that provided mom and dad with enough to pay off the house and still give them money to live on. Now, Dad is eighty-one and mom is eighty and both of them are diabetics."

"Okay, I will call the Sheriff and let him know we need to see how they are doing," I said as I picked up the phone.

The phone on the other end of the line rang several times before someone finally answered, "Sheriff's Office,"

"Hi, this is Detective Calvin York of the CBI. Is the Sheriff in?"

"No, he hasn't made it in yet. We have just been hit with at least thirty inches of snow yesterday and last night and no one is moving very well yet. The Sheriff called me early this morning and said he was going to get his snow mobile going this morning and will be in late. Do you want him to call you when he gets in?" A woman on the line asked. "Yes, that would be great. My number is 555—875-7516," I told the lady on the other end of the line.

I hung up the phone and said, "The Sheriff's Office just said they have just had thirty inches of snow the last day and a half and everyone is not moving very fast today. He will call me when he gets into his office. Now tell me a little more about your father and mother."

"Well as I said, my father worked at the mine as did his father and his grandfather. His grandfather started working shortly after the mine was opened in 1887 and his father started in 1904. Dad started working at the mine as soon as he graduated from Battle Mountain High School in 1932. It was the only job he could get during the depression and he worked until the EPA closed it down in 1986. Since he was only fifty-four years old at that time, he moved to Red Cliff and worked as a mechanic. While working at the mine he started as a miner's helpers putting dynamite into the holes drilled by the miner. Later, after several years he was elevated to a miner and then after another period of time he started working at the grinder down by the river. He ended his career as a foreman of the loading crew who loaded the ore into train cars. You should look up the Gilman

The Ghost of Gilman

Mine on Google. There is a lot of information there that is very interesting." She related.

"Were you and your brother born at Gilman?" I asked.

"Yes, we both were born there. We went to grade school in the school house, had fun at the Club House with a number of other young children and really enjoyed our early life in Gilman. We both went to high school in Minturn at Battle Mountain High School before it was relocated to Eagle. After high school, we both went to college here in Denver where we stayed with dad's sister. I am now an instructor in English at Denver Junior College and Al is an attorney in Colorado Springs. Al is as worried as I am," She said. "Dad always told us he wanted to die in Gilman since there were already so many Ghosts already there."

"I guess you were smart enough to get out of that mining community since you both have very rewarding jobs," I replied.

Just then, my phone rang. I picked it up and said, "Hello, this is Detective York. Can I help you?"

"Yes, Detective York, this is Sheriff Jameson of Eagle County. I was told you have a problem that needs my attention," the Sheriff replied.

I explained the situation to him and then said, "I was hoping you could have one of your deputies check on the Wise house since neither their daughter nor their son can get in touch with them and are worried."

The Sheriff said, "I have a deputy stationed in Minturn and I will see if he can get up to Red Cliff. That road is very high and may be impassable due to the deep snow we have just had but I will get him started. He may have to use his snow machine to get there. I will keep you posted on what we find out."

"Okay, I will stay in my office until I hear from you. Please let me know as soon as possible since both of these people are in their eighties and may need some medical help. Their daughter is here with me. I will let her know what your deputy finds out when you call me. She also has said, they both are diabetics, so she is very worried," I explained to the Sheriff."

The Ghost of Gilman

Chapter 2

Joyce suggested. "Joan, I think you should go back home and let Cal do his magic as he calls it.   I will call you there when he gets any information."

"Okay," Joan said. "I think I should call Al and let him know what we are doing. He may want to come up here to talk with you as well."

I looked at Joan and replied, "That would be great if he could come here.   Just let him know where I'm at. I don't know how I-25 is with all the snow so have him call me if he is coming."

The Ghost of Gilman

"Okay," she said as she stood and got ready to leave my office, "Please call me as soon as you hear anything."

"I will Joan. Just relax and we will find out where they are," I told her as I walked and Joyce to the door.

Joyce escorted her back down to the bottom floor of the CBI building. When she returned, she came into my office and said, "I saw Sidney come in while I was in the reception area and told him what you are doing. He said he would check with you later today."

I decided to take Joan's suggestion and Googled Gilman Mine. Wikipedia reported: 'The Gilman Mines were founded in 1886 during the Colorado Silver Boom, the town later became a center of lead and zinc mining in Colorado, on the now-flooded Eagle Mine. It was abandoned in 1986 by order of the Environmental Protection Agency since it was contaminating river and ground water, as well as unprofitability of the mines. It is currently a ghost town on private property and is strictly off limits to the public. At the time of the abandonment, the mining operations were owned by Viacom

International. As of 2007, The Ginn Company has plans to build a private ski resort with private home sites across Battle Mountain --- including development at the Gilman townsite. On February 27, 2008 the Minturn Town Council unanimously approved annexation and development plans for 4,300 acres (6.7 square miles) of Ginn Resorts' 1,700-unit Battle Mountain residential ski and golf resort; Ginn's Battle Mountain development includes much of the old Gilman townsite. On May 20, 2008 the town of Minturn approved the annexation in a public referendum with 87% of the vote. As of September 9, 2009 the Ginn Company has backed out of development plans for the Battle Mountain Property. Crave Real Estate Ventures who was the original finance to Ginn will now take over day to day operations of the property.

The town sits at an elevation of 8950 ft (2,700 m) on a dramatic 600-foot (180 m) cliff above the Eagle River on the flank of Battle Mountain. It is located southeast of Minturn and north of Tennessee Pass

along U.S. Highway 24. The remnants of the townsite are visible in many places along the curves of the highway. More recent housing situated on the steep flank of the mountain itself near the former mines.

This mining district once was the richest and most successful in Eagle County. The ore occurs in sulfide replacement deposits of three types: 1) thin-bedded deposits in the Sawatch Quartzite, (2) highly elongated ore bodies in the Leadville Limestone (here completely dolomitized), and (3) vertical pipes or chimneys cutting across the various formations. The ore minerals in order of decreasing abundance are sphalerite, chalcopyrite, and galena. The non-ore minerals pyrite and siderite are also very abundant in the ore bodies.

Several mining operations had sprouted along Battle Mountain by 1879, the first year of the Colorado Silver Boom. The town of Gilman and nearby mining operations were developed in the 1880s by John Clinton, a prospector, judge, and speculator from nearby Red Cliff. In 1887, gold and silver were discovered in two vertical chimneys at the Ground Hog Mine, which continued to produce gold and silver ore until the 1920s. In the 1880s, Clinton acquired a number of mining operations in the vicinity, including the profitable Iron Mask, noted for its numerous caverns with crystal formations. Clinton developed the area as a town and improved the mining operations with higher capitalization. The town, which Clinton developed in order to keep miners at the site, was initially named for him. He donated the land for its initial schoolhouse and built its first boarding house. Later the name of the mine was changed to Gilman. **The Denver and Rio Grande Railroad** reached the mining camp of Gilman at the base of the cliff in 1882. By 1899, Gilman had a population of approximately 300, as well as a newspaper, called the *Gilman Enterprise.*

As they reached the deeper primary sulfide ores, the miners found that the ore contained so much zinc that the smelters refused to buy it. A roaster and magnetic separator were installed in 1905 to separate out the zinc minerals, turning the problem into an asset. The mining operations transitioned increasingly to zinc, although the Eagle Mine was still the leading producer of silver in the state in 1930.

When the **New Jersey Zinc** entered Gilman in 1912, they operated the mine over a period of years and purchased all the principal mines and the entire townsite. Zinc was the economic mainstay until 1931, when low zinc prices forced the company to switch to mining copper-silver ores. Zinc production resumed in 1941, and remained the principal product of the mines until they were closed in the 1980s.

The town population was a few hundred in the 1960s. At one time, the town had an infirmary, grocery store, and bowling alley. The town experienced labor strife several times in the 1950s, partly inflamed by the out-of-state corporate ownership. By 1970, total production at the mines was 10 million tons of ore; 393,000 troy ounces of gold; 66,000,000 ounces of silver; 105,000 tons of copper; 148,000 tons of lead; and 858,000 tons of zinc.

After the closure of the mine and the abandonment of the town, a 235-acre area, which included 8 million tons of mine waste, were designated a Superfund site by the EPA and placed on the National Priorities List in 1986.

During the early 20th century, the mining operations transitioned increasingly to zinc, although the Eagle Mine was still the leading producer of silver in the state in 1930. The mining district became the richest and most successful in Eagle County. Between the 1940s and 1980s, zinc was the principal product of the mines. By the 1980s the mining operations had become unprofitable and the ground water contaminated. In 1984 Gilman was abandoned by order of the of toxic pollutants. Since then the town has been vandalized and the main street has been heavily tagged. It is said that there are no intact windows left anywhere in the city anymore. However, many parts of the town remain almost as they were when the mine shut down. There is a large sign on the locked gate leading to the old ghost town that reads, no trespassing. People are subjected to a One-thousand-dollar fine if they trespass. This was signed by the Sheriff of Eagle County.

I then looked at a map of the area and discovered the gate to Gilman was about four miles north of Red Cliff on US-24 and about six miles south of Minturn, Colorado. The gate is on the top of a high barren ridge just south of a large switchback in the highway that climbs from near the base of the canyon that sits at 7900 feet to almost 9000 feet.

I explored Google Earth and zoomed in until

The Ghost of Gilman

I could see the abandon houses and the layout of the town. I thought to myself, I would like to go there just to see the old ghost town, but I would need the Sheriff's permission.

I had just shut off my computer after I had printed off all of the information I had found on Gilman and sat back reviewing the information when Sidney walked into my office.

"Okay Cal, what have you gotten yourself into now?" he asked with a smile on his face.

I explained my visit this morning with Joan Ault and informed him I had contacted the Sheriff of Eagle County to see if he could assist in getting any information on the old couple.

As I concluded my explanation, my phone rang. I picked it up and recognized Sheriff Jameson voice, "Detective York, my deputy in Minturn said the road to Red Cliff would not be open for at least a day or more, but he knows a man in Red Cliff and asked him to go to the Wise's home to check on them. He just got back to me. The man in Red Cliff, by the name of Sam James, went up to their house. It wasn't even locked, and it was completely empty. He went in, looked around, and didn't find anything of interest until he looked into the refrigerator. When he opened the door, he saw two packages of insulin with the names of William Wise and Wilma Wise. They had been used since each syringe was about half gone. It almost looks like someone either took them or they just left. As soon as I can, I will personally go down to Red Cliff and look around. In the meantime, I have put out a missing person report to all agencies in this area. Sam James told me he personally knows both Bill and Wilma Wise. He said Bill always join a bunch of friends in Red Cliff for coffee every morning, but they haven't seen either of them for at least five or six days."

How far south of Minturn is the Gate to Gilman?" I asked.

"It is about five and a half miles. Sam said they have about forty inches of snow on the level in Red Cliff. My best guess on when the road will be opened is probably two days." Sheriff Jameson replied.

"Is there a place where we I can rent a snow mobile in Minturn?" I inquired.

"The closest place you could rent a snow mobile and trailer would be in Vail. There

31

are two places I know of there where they are available," the Sheriff replied and then asked, "Are you thinking about going up to Gilman on a snow mobile?"

"Yes, it crossed my mind particularly under the circumstances of them be diabetic. I've had a recent experience with someone who was diabetic, and they would definitely need some help," I said.

"Well if you do, let me know. I may just go with you," Jameson replied. "I think I would enjoy going with you."

Since I had my phone on the speaker, Sidney had heard everything and then said, "I would also like to take that trip with Cal."

Sheriff Jameson reacted, "Is that you Sidney. I haven't seen you in ages. Why don't we set something up for tomorrow. Can you be here by noon?"

Sidney answered, "Yes, if I-70 is cleared by tonight. Cal and I will leave early tomorrow morning and will meet you at the Vail Police Station. Can you go ahead and get us three good snow mobiles?"

"Sure, and I'll tell Chief Dunny you are coming over on this mission. I know he thinks a lot of you," Sheriff Jameson said. "I'll see you tomorrow."

"Well that idea certainly snowballed in a matter of speaking," I said smiling. "I need to get me a snow mobile suit and boots. Do you have one?" I asked Sidney.

"Yes, I have a couple and since we are both about the same size, you can use one of mine. All you need then is a pair of warm water proof boots," Sidney replied.

I thought about what he had said and then responded, "Well I have some good hunting packs that are waterproof and warm. I think I could get by with those."

"Yes, they will work well. Meet me here tomorrow morning at five thirty. Normally it only takes two hours to get to Vail, but with this snow it will probably take us longer. I will check out a Yukon for our trip. You just bring what you need, and we will head west," Sidney instructed.

Before I left, I called Joan and informed her of our activities for the next couple of days. She asked me to keep her informed on what we find in Gilman. I said I would work through Joyce and she would make sure everything was provided.

I then went home and started packing for the trip over to Vail. Mary became worried and said, "I've been watching the local news of this snow storm and they say the mountain passes are closed at both Eisenhower Tunnel and Vail Pass. Will you still go if they remain closed?"

"No, Sidney is monitoring the road conditions both on I-70 and US-24 to see if they become open and stay open. If they remain closed, we will just call the Sheriff and tell him we will wait until we can get there."

"What do you think happened to those two old people?" Mary probed my thought process as only she could.

I replied knowing she was nervous. "Once we find them, we can determine what the circumstances of their disappearance."

"Well come on into the kitchen. I have our dinner ready and then I think you should go to bed early since you will be getting up early tomorrow."

Chapter 3

When I drove into the CBI parking lot the next morning, Sidney had the big Yukon parked outside the front door. I went up to his office to see if he was there, but I didn't see anyone. When I got back down to the Reception Lobby, he was standing there looking outside at the weather.

"Did you hear the weather report this morning?" He asked.

"Yes," I responded. "The radio station I was listening to on the way to work said we should have light snow here this morning and clearing this afternoon. Is that what you heard?

"Yes, that is what I heard for the Denver Area too, but I also checked some of the mountain towns. They indicate they expect more snow today. Therefore, I think we should go ahead and if it gets too bad, we will just turn around and come home," Sidney said as he climbed under the steering wheel of the Yukon.

As we headed west, the sun broke out and it was a very bright day. The highway crews had cleared the road surface well. As we neared Eisenhower Tunnel, there was a small amount of snow between the two tracks the tires of cars make on the road surface. Emerging from the tunnel and driving down toward Silverthorne the road was again clear.

We didn't hit any snow on the road until we started up Vail Pass. About five miles past Copper Mountain, there was a State Patrol car blocking west bound traffic. There were about twenty cars parked in front of us. We stopped and walked up to the Patrolman. Sidney showed him his badge and said, "We have to get to Vail Police Station as soon as possible this morning. Will the pass be opened soon?"

The Patrolman replied, "Yes, we have two or three snow plows heading this way. There is about three feet of snow on top of the pass and when they get here, you go ahead and pull ahead of all of these cars and follow him down to Vail. From there, the roads are all open now."

"Okay, thanks for the information. Do you know when the plows will be here?" Sidney asked.

"They should be here in about thirty minutes. Sorry but you know how this works. We are just trying to get this road open and it all takes time."

We went back to the Yukon and started pulling around the line of cars. People started getting out of their cars yelling at us for passing them so Sidney said, "Roll down you window and hold your badge out so they can see we are Law Officers."

I did as he instructed and the people who were ahead of us started getting back in their cars when they say my badge.

After a short cold wait, I saw the two plows

coming down the pass throwing snow over six feet high off the road.

When the snow plows approached the road block, they pulled into a cross over and a line of cars heading east started down the pass. We followed the snow plows all the way to the eastern edge of Vail where the road again became passable.

I looked at my watch as we pulled up to the Vail Police Station and noticed it was now about ten o'clock.

When we entered, the receptionist said as she saw our badges, "Chief Dunny is waiting for you. Sheriff Jameson is already here. His office is the first on your left."

We walked down a corridor and knocked on the Chief's door. Hearing the command, "Come in," we opened the door to a large office. The Chief and the Sheriff were sitting at a long conference table looking at a map of Eagle County.

The Chief motioned us to a seat at the table and said, "You both look like you could use some coffee."

Before Sidney could answer, I said, "Yes that would be great. We just survived the snowy road over Vail Pass, and I need something to quiet my nerves."

The Chief smiled as he picked up his phone and said, "Can you bring another pot of coffee into my office?"

Within a minute, the receptionist came into the room and set a big pot of coffee down along with some sweet rolls.

We immediately started looking at the map up to Gilman. The Chief looked at both of us and said, "I have just talked with the road crews who are working on US-24 and they say they probably won't have the road open until sometime tomorrow. The Sheriff has explained why you are here, and I have three snow mobiles on trailers out back. You can take them down to Minturn and unload them. Then you will have to travel the five and a half miles from there to the gate to Gilman. I did have an airplane fly over that area early this morning and they reported there is a car parked at the gate. It is an old car they thought looked like a 1967 Chevrolet. Do you think that may be their car?"

I tried to remember if Joan had told me what

kind of car her parents had but nothing came to mind. "I can call someone and find out. If it is not their car, then we might not have to go all the way up there."

The Chief nodded his concurrence. I fished out my cell phone and punched in Joan's number.

When she answered, I asked her, "What kind of car does your parents have?"

She replied quickly, "They drive an old car. I think it is a Chevrolet, but I don't know cars very well. Have you found something?"

"No, not yet," I replied not wanting to get her too excited. "I am still in Vail and am about ready to take a snowmobile up to Gilman. I will let you know what we find up there."

The Chief smiled and said, "You know Cal, you won't be able to use your cell phone up in Gilman. I hope you brought a SAT phone with you."

Chief, I replied, "I always have a SAT phone with me. On previous cases in remote places I have had to use it often."

Sheriff Jameson looked at both of us and said, "I think we should get something to eat before we go. We have no idea how long we will be out, so we need to eat first. Let's go down to the local café and get something."

Sidney replied, "Good idea Sheriff. I saw a little café on the way here next to I-70. Why don't we hook up the trailers and head over there. That way we can just leave from there. Chief, I want to thank you for those snow mobiles. I had planned to rent some, but this is even better. I will also keep you informed on our progress as we start up the hill. I don't want to become stranded out there overnight."

"Yes, that is a good idea Sheriff. The weather forecast for tonight is temperatures below zero. I would suggest you have your deputy in Minturn stand by in case you need to be rescued. I think this could be a dangerous mission, but I also understand why you want to get these old people out of there."

After a pleasant meal, we headed for Minturn where we met Deputy Milken and gave him instructions. The Sheriff gave him his SAT phone in case we needed to get in touch with him.

At that time, we all put on our heavy snow suits and boots. I pulled a big stocking cap

The Ghost of Gilman

down over my head before I put on my helmet. Sidney looked at me and said, "That was good thinking Cal. I wish I had thought of bringing a stocking cap as well. The Sheriff reached into his big back pack and pulled out another one and gave it to Sidney.

The Sheriff smiled as Sidney pulled it down over his ears and said, "I always have two of everything when I'm out here in the winter. I guess you city slickers don't usually need them."

Sidney just nodded at that comment as he started his snow machine.

The first part of the trip on US-24 was easy going. There was only about a foot of snow for the first mile of so as we traveled along the Eagle River. The snow became deeper as we entered a steep canyon. By the time the Sheriff pointed out a road sign designating Road 707, the snow was estimated to be three feet deep.

We stopped for a little while and had a drink of hot coffee from a thermos the Sheriff had filled at the café and then headed on up the highway. As I sipped the hot coffee, I looked over at Sidney and said, "You look good with a snow beard."

Rod Beach

Sidney wiped his face with his glove and a big mass of snow came off. "You look good in one as well." He said.

The going became more difficult as we skimmed along snowbanks and drifts across the highway for another two miles. The Sheriff who was leading stopped again at a bridge that crossed the Eagle River and said, "This is where we will start climbing up toward the top of a high ridge. This climb is about two miles long and there are trees on both sides of the road so the snow will be deeper on this stretch."

The snow machines were working hard climbing the steep hill and around a couple of switchbacks. When we got through the trees, the ridge was visible, and the depth of the snow was much less. We made better time for the next mile but the wind on the ridge was strong and cold.

We then came to another climb and the Sheriff stopped again and said, "Ahead of us is a long switch back that is steep and curvy but doesn't have any trees along the side. So, the wind reduces the amount on snow on the road. When we get to the top of this climb and around the final curve, we will be at the gate to Gilman."

I breathed a sigh of relief. I was getting colder and wetter as we continued up the big switchback. As we rounded the last big curve in the road, I saw a car sitting in front of a steel gate across the entrance road to Gilman that included a large four-foot sign that read:

NO TRESSPASSING

VIOLATORS WILL BE FINED $1000

The Sheriff pulled up to the gate and we pulled up beside him. I could see three rows of old houses about two hundred yards in front of me.

I turned to Sheriff Jameson as I pointed to the old houses and said, "I expected many more houses that these."

"Oh, these houses were the Barrio area. The mine owners went down to Mexico and hired a large number of Mexicans to work in the mine. These houses were for them. If you look further up the mountain, you can see some trees and some more buildings. That is where all the white miners lived as well as all of the supporting buildings are."

Rod Beach

Sidney looked at me and said, "I guess back in the day, there was more discrimination of different people."

I just nodded and then asked the Sheriff, "Do we have to walk from here?"

"No, I have a key to the lock. I will unlock it and we can drive our snowmobiles all the way into the town."

"Okay, that sounds great but first I want to check out their car<" I said as I walked back toward the old Chevrolet. I scrapped the snow off the windows and looked into the car. I tried the door and discovered it was unlocked so I opened it and looked around finding nothing. Satisfied I went back to the gate where the Sheriff was unlocking it at the time.

When he unlocked the gate, it swung open wide. We climbed back on our snowmobiles and he then lead us up a small slope and into the middle of the town. When he stopped, he said, "That building over there was their bowling ally and clubhouse. They even had a small basketball court that doubled as a dance floor. Then those houses over in the trees were where the big shots lived. They had all the comforts of any place around these parts. Those houses over there," He said pointing at three rows of nice wooden houses, "were for the white miners."

"Joan said she and her brother both went to grade school up here. Where is the school house?" I asked.

"Oh, they tore that down a long time ago. It was a really nice school house and some of the people used the lumber of that place to build their homes elsewhere," the Sheriff replied.

Sidney looked at me and asked, "Where do you think we should start looking for your old couple?"

"I don't know. They could be anywhere. Why don't we split up and start looking into all of the houses and other buildings until we find them. If either of you find them just fire your weapon up in the air and we can then all come to that location," I said as I looked at the other two.

The Sheriff replied, "That sounds like a good plan. I will start with the big homes and you two should take a look at both sides of the street. They could be anywhere.

As I walked around, I noticed the people who lived here left in a hurry. They left many things that many people would take with them when they moved. There were many toys in the houses, old iron beds, old moldy blankets, ironing boards, and many other personal items. In some of the offices, papers were strewn over the floors and in one building, an old washing machine still stood.

I looked into every building along my side of the main street and never found any thing that would show the two old people had been there. I finally arrived at the end of the street and saw a large cinder block building. I went into it and discovered it was the medical building. There were x-rays scattered all over the floor in one room and in another area was a big laboratory complete with glass beakers and other scientific equipment. This building was built to last much longer than the wooden homes. As I started to exit this builidng, I saw Sidney and Sheriff Jameson walking through the deep snow toward me. I stayed inside the building since it kept me out of the cold wind that was blowing across the high ridge. When they stepped inside the building out of the wind, Sidney said, "Man, I am cold. Do you think we can start a small fire and warm

The Ghost of Gilman

up a little while we discuss what we didn't find?"

The Sheriff quickly replied rubbing his hands together to keep them warm. "I will go get some old wood and if you can get some of those papers in a pile, we can start a small fire inside this building. We will have to be careful not to let it get out of hand, but I would like to warm up as well."

I gathered some old papers out of an office area that consisted of medical records of different miners, crumpled them up and scraped away an area on the concrete floor. The Sheriff returned with an armful of old wooden planks and we built a small fire. As we sat around the warm fire, we discussed what we didn't find.

Sidney said, "I never saw anything during my search of the north side homes that would indicate anyone had used the area for many years."

"Neither did I," the Sheriff added.

"While I was looking around in this building, I started thinking what Joan told me yesterday. She said, she had not heard from them for almost a week or more. What was the weather like last week up here Sheriff?"

Rod Beach

"It was pleasant. This is the first big snow we have had this winter. It snowed some time ago, but it has been nice and warm the last two weeks before yesterday?"

"Well if it was nice, maybe they drove up here and had trouble with their car and called someone to take them back to Red Cliff. That is why we haven't seen any foot prints or any other sign of them being here." I said.

Sidney considered what I said. "Why don't you call Joan and ask her if they have called her yet?"

I reached into my back pack and pulled out my SAT phone and dialed Joan's number. When she answered, I asked, "Joan, this is Detective York. Has your parents called you yet?"

"No" she answered. "Why are you asking me that?"

"Well, I am up in Gilman right now in about two feet of snow and there is no sign of them here. Do you have any idea where they would go up here?"

"They could be almost anywhere. I know my dad always missed the place where he worked at just before he retired and always said he would like to go back and visit it."

"Where would that place be?" I asked.

"The last place he worked was at the loading building. That is where the coal was taken to be loaded onto coal trains. That building was next to the ore processing facility at the bottom of the canyon. He was the foreman there. It is located at the bottom of the cliff next to the old train tracks,"

"Is there any way to get down there from the Where we are," I asked.

"There used to be a steep set of wooden stairs that he used to walk up and down but I'm sure they have decayed by now. I also know there is a narrow steep trail along the side of the cliff, but it is very dangerous to go that way. The easiest way is to go down to Red Cliff and follow the old train tracks up to where the coal was loaded."

"Okay, I guess we will have to check that out," I said as I switch off my SAT Phone.

I repeated what she had related to me and said, "Sheriff, do you know a way down to the train tracks from here?"

Rod Beach

"I can show you the old stairs they built for that purpose, but I wouldn't want to try to go that way down. I think I would rather take the snowmobiles down to Red Cliff and then up the train tracks. That would be much safer," he replied.

"Yes, that is what Joan suggested as well. Let's sit here for a little while to get warm and then let's head for Red Cliff. I think it will be an interesting trip."

The Sheriff nodded his head and exclaimed, "Yes, it is down hill most of the way. However, the Highway Road Crews are working on that end of the highway so some of it may even be cleared. We will probably need our snowmobiles to go up the train tracks so somehow we will need to get them down to Red Cliff since the highway may not have enough snow on it that will allow us to use them."

Sidney looked at both of us and said, "Let's worry about that when we need to. It is now about three o'clock, so we need to get going. It will be getting dark around four thirty."

The Ghost of Gilman

Chapter 4

We made our way back to our snowmobiles and drove out the gate and stopped so the Sheriff could lock it again. We then turned right and headed down the mountain on the snow- covered Highway 24. The snow on the road was as deep here as it was on the way up the mountain. After traveling at a slow pace for about four miles, the road took us around a sharp curve down into a deep cut along the edge of a rock cliff. The right edge of the road where the guard rail on the edge of the road was almost buried with snow. We had to be careful since if we ran over the guard rail, we would careen off the road and crash down a very steep wall of rock. Finally,

The Ghost of Gilman

after about an hour of careful driving, we rounded a curve and saw the signpost with 709 Road on it and pointing toward Red Cliff off to the left. At this time the road was only covered with a thin coat of snow, but it was still enough to allow the snowmobiles to skid along smoothly. We went east about a half mile before we entered Red Cliff. Looking back toward US-24 I saw a magnificent steel gartered bridge spanning the canyon where Red Cliff was nestled in. The Sheriff led the way up to the Green Bridge Inn. "I don't want to tell you how to run your investigation, but I do know it is going to be dark very soon and it will get extremely cold since the sky doesn't have a cloud in it tonight. I suggest we get a room for the night here, and maybe go up to the house where the old man and wife lived and check it out for any clues."

"Sheriff, that is probably the wisest thing I've heard today. I think I need to warm up, but I also think checking out their house would be good. Do you think we can ride the snowmobiles up to their house?"

"Yes, there is enough snow on these streets to do that easily, but first let's get our rooms before they sell out," the Sheriff replied.

Rod Beach

I looked up and saw a three-story hotel with twenty-six rooms on each of the top two floors and a number of small stores on the bottom. I looked at him and said, "So you think they may not have a room for us?"

"You never know. This is a great place and the scenery is outstanding. Maybe some visitors are stranded up here since they didn't leave before the big snow hit. Let's go in and see," the Sheriff replied.

As we walked into the hotel, the older woman behind the counter came out and ran up to Sheriff Jameson. She gave him a big hug and a kiss and said, "Jason, it is so good to see you again. What brings you to Red Cliff on this fine day?"

The Sheriff turned to us and said, "This is Sidney Kingsbury, Chief of Investigations of the Colorado Bureau of Investigations and this is Detective Calvin York. We are up here trying to locate William and Wilma Wise. Their daughter in Denver is worried since they haven't called her in over a week. Alice, have you seen either of them around town?"

"No, as a matter of fact I haven't. They weren't even in church last Sunday. It was such a nice day I just thought they probably went on a picnic," she replied. "Have you been up to their house yet?"

"No, we just came over the mountain on some snowmobiles and pulled into town," The Sheriff replied and then said. We need three rooms for the night. Do you have any available?"

"Well, I think I have only five available tonight.

I have had three parties stranded here last night and there are a number of others who are spending at least a week up here site-seeing. Do you want one of the available ones?" She recited as she looked at Sidney and me.

The Sheriff replied, "Yes and just put them on the County's bill. We will be back as soon as we get through looking at the Wise's house."

The Sheriff looked at me smiling as we climbed onto the snowmobiles and said, "You can't always judge a hotel by where it is located."

We drove down the canyon on Water Street. After two blocks the Sheriff turned off onto South Water Street and stopped in front of a nicely painted white bungalow with a garage behind it.

We all climbed off our respective machines and walked up to the covered front porch. We stomped the snow off our boots, opened the door and walked into a small but nicely decorated living room. There was a copy of the Denver Post sitting on the coffee table in front of a nice couch. The date on the paper was six days ago. I went into the kitchen and opened the refrigerator and saw two half full tubes of insulin and two different syringes complete with small needles. Obviously, both Bill and Wilma were on insulin and after five or six days they would be in extreme conditions. Without it.

Sidney and I went into the master bedroom that again was well kept. We didn't see anything there that would indicate where they could be. We then went into the other bedroom. This room had an unmade bed and a bunch of dirty clothes stuffed into the corner of the closet. There was an ash tray full of spent cigarettes. Looking closer into the closet, I saw a half empty bottle of Jim Beam whiskey. I remembered Joan telling me her father and mother neither drank or smoked. I wondered who had used this room lately. I called Sidney to come into this bedroom and when he did, he was as astonished as I was. "We need to find out who is sleeping in this room," he said.

"Maybe the Sheriff knows."

We called the Sheriff into the messy bedroom and showed him what I had discovered. I asked him, "Do you know if they rented this room out to a border?"

"I have no idea but maybe Alice will know," he replied.

We rummaged around for another fifteen minutes but never found anything that would help. As I was getting ready to leave, I stopped by the telephone and saw a hand-written note. 'call Andy'. I picked up the note and put it into my pocket.

We left the house but before we got onto our snowmobiles, I decided to look into the garage. When I opened the big overhead door, I saw an almost complete wood working system and several shelves and a nice table that had been build but remained unpainted or stained. I wondered about that. Then I saw another note on his work bench. I picked it up and read a dull penciled note that read "Talk with Sam to see if he knows Joe Sample.'

I took both notes out and showed them to Sidney and Sheriff Jameson. "What do you make out of these notes?"

Sheriff Jameson looked at the note I found in the garage and said, "I don't know who this Sam is, but I do know Joe Sample. He is a bum who has been arrested numerous times for robbery, assault, drunkenness, and many other causes. He is a bad apple. I know he lives in Minturn most of the time, but our department has arrested him in Vail, Eagle, Minturn but never in Red Cliff. He may be living up here now. Let's ask Alice about his as well. She may also know this guy by the name of Sam who seems to be sleeping in the Wise's spare bedroom."

We climbed back onto our snowmobiles and headed back to the Mountain View Hotel. When we walked in Alice met us at the counter and handed each of us a key to a second story room. The Sheriff looked at her and said, "Alice, do you know if Joe Sample lives here in Red Cliff now?"

"Yes, he is renting a cabin on the outskirts of town. He spends most of his time with a bunch of guys at the 'Never Closed Bar' down the street. That bar just opened last summer and always has a bunch of bikers and hard looking men there. I guess Joe fits in well. I don't let him into my hotel any more since he wrecked a room last year."

"Yes, I remember that arrest. He spent two weeks in the Eagle County Jail for that offense. The Sheriff replied turning to us as he spoke. He then turned back to Alice and said, "Now, there seems to be someone staying at the Wise's house in their spare bedroom. Do you know who that might be?"

"Yes, his name is Sam Wilcox. He moved to Red Cliff last summer and works for the Union Lumber Company cutting trees in the forest. He cuts the trees and they haul them down here to be made into plywood. Wilma Wise told me at church they were renting their spare bedroom to him so they could get a little more money each month. I have only met him once, but he seems like a nice man. However, I also think you are a nice man as well," she said laughing.

"Okay, that is enough of that kind of talk," the Sheriff said jokingly. "Now, do you know someone who goes by the name of Andy?"

Rod Beach

"The only Andy I know is Andy Alvarez. He is a retired or I guess fired miner who worked for Bill Wise when the mine was closed."

I asked, "Do you know why Andy was fired?"

"If I remember correctly, he was caught steeling tools from the mine. He was a close friend of Bill and when Bill reported the missing tools, the Company fired him. He moved down to Minturn a year or two ago," Alice relied.

We then each went to our assigned rooms. My room was on the front of the hotel looking down on the maid street. The room was very nicely furnished with a queen-sized bed, a nice bathroom complete with a shower, and even a television set.

I spent a few minutes writing down what we had done today and what we had discovered at the Wise's house into my notebook. I made a note to myself to try to find Joe Sample, Sam Wilcox, and this Andy Alvarez. After I did that, I went down to the lobby and soon Sidney joined me. We sat alone in the lobby talking when Sidney looked up saying,

"I wonder where Alice is?"

We sat and waited for about twenty minutes

until the Sheriff came down to join us. His face was red, and he seemed to be out of breath. "Are you guys ready for a good dinner tonight?"

"Yes, I am starving," Sidney replied. "Where do you suggest we go?"

"There is Jaquan's Bar and Grill. People come over here from Vail and Beavercreek just to eat his great food. He serves both Mexican and American food and it is quite good. I think you will like it," Jameson replied. "For some reason, I am very hungry tonight. Then tomorrow morning we can go up the railroad tracks about three miles to the ore processing area and check that out. Does Jaquan's sound alright with you?"

"Yes," Sidney responded before I could. "I think it is probably the only place in town isn't it?

"Yes, you are right, but it is a good place to eat," the Sheriff responded laughing.

We walked down the street about a hundred yards and saw a small deep building next to a larger wooden structure that housed a hardware store. When we entered, we were greeted by a man who obviously knew the

Sheriff. He gave the Sheriff a big hug and said, "Who are you bringing me tonight?"

"These are two detectives from Denver. We are here trying to find the Wise family. Have you seen then recently?"

"No, Bill usually stops in every morning for coffee with the other old guys, but he hasn't been here for at least six or seven days. Do you think something happen to him?" Jaquan asked.

"We don't know. They seem to be missing and we are trying to find them. Their daughter is worried they haven't called her in over a week, so they wanted these detectives to try to find them. Now do you have a table for us?" The Sheriff said.

"Yes Sir, please follow me," he said as he lead us toward the back of the bar. He came back shortly with our menus and asked would you like your usual beer Sheriff?

"Yes, I will start with a tall one of my favorite drinks," the Sheriff answered. Jaquan turned to us and said, "Would you like something to drink?"

Sidney answered first while I was still looking at the detailed menu. He said, "I would like a double Jack Daniels with a lemon."

"Very good choice sir and what you like," He said looking at me.

"Can you fix me a tall margarita?" I said.

"Another good choice. Would you like salt on the rim," he asked.

I just nodded.

While he was fixing our drinks, Sidney asked Jameson, "What would you recommend to eat here?"

"I always start with a bowl of his chili. It will warm you up. Then I order a Riley Burger with a slice of pineapple and onion rings. His burgers are all just great, but I really like the Riley," the Sheriff replied.

I looked at Sidney and said, "That sounds good to me."

When Jaquan brought our drinks he asked, "Have you decided what you want to eat?"

The Sheriff gave him his order and Sidney and I just said, "We'll have the same."

We sat and I started reviewing what I had put into my notebook. Both Sidney and the Sheriff agreed with my assessment. The

Rod Beach

Sheriff then said, "Well, first we have to find the two. I am starting to think they may be dead somewhere. After a week without their insulin, they may have just died. I hope tomorrow we can find them at the loading shed next to the ore processing center."

"Yes, I hope so too, but I'm hoping they may still be alive."

The Ghost of Gilman

Chapter 5

After a good night sleep, I woke rubbing my eyes, took a quick shower and called Mary. When I met Sidney in the hotel lobby, I asked, "Did you call your wife this morning?"

Sidney jumped up, pulled out his cell phone and walked away dialing his wife's number. He spent about five minutes talking with her and then came back where I was waiting for the Sheriff to arrive.

"I know I always make sure you call Mary, so I guess it is only fair you had to tell me to call Arlene. She was happy to talk with me.

After waiting for well over twenty minutes,

The Ghost of Gilman

Sheriff Jameson finally arrived. His face was again red and sweaty for such a cold mourning. I looked at Sidney and he was just shaking his head back and forth.

Sidney asked, "Sheriff, is there a place here where we can get a big breakfast. I think we may not be anywhere where we can get a lunch, so I want to stock up of some food to fight the cold weather this morning. We should also fill up our gas tanks on the snowmobiles."

The Sheriff replied laughing. "First there is no gas stations in Red Cliff. The nearest is in Minturn or Vail. Red Cliff does not have any places for breakfast but fear not. I know a guy that has a one-thousand-gallon gasoline barrel and he always let's me fill my tank when I'm down here. Then, since Jaquan lives in the rear of his bar and grill, I think he will make a breakfast for us. Let's stop by there first and place our orders and then we will go see Leland and buy some gasoline from him. Would that be okay with you."

Sidney holding back a laugh said, "Yes, that would be great. I think we should get going since we have a lot of work to do today."

Rod Beach

We went outside to our snowmobiles, brushed a little blown snow off and climbed on and drove over to Jaquan's Bar and Grill. We walked around the side of the building to a door and the Sheriff knocked. Soon, the door open and there stood Jaquan dressed in a white tee shirt and ragged blue jeans. He rubbed his eyes and looked at the Sheriff. "I would guess, you guys would like some breakfast. What do you want to eat. I can fry some bacon and whip up a batch of pancakes if that would be okay."

The Sheriff replied, "Thanks, that would be great. We are going down to Leland's house and buy some gasoline for our snowmobiles so we will be back in about fifteen minutes. Will that give you enough time?"

"Yes, that would be great. I will also put a pot of coffee on so you can take some with you this morning. It is supposed to be really cold today," he said as the walked away from the door closing it behind him.

The Sheriff lead the way down the street toward the bottom of he town. He pulled his snowmobile in next to a small barn, got off, and went up to the back door of a small old house. The door open and we saw him motioning toward us and the snowmobiles. The man closed his door and the Sheriff started walking back toward where we sat on our snowmobiles.

"Leland said, he would sell us some gasoline. His barrel is almost empty, but he thinks the truck from Vail will be able to make it over the hill this afternoon. I guess, the road crews are clearing that road before US-24 since more people from Vail come here than from Minturn. You know the hotel rate is much lower here than in Vail, so some people stay here and drive the twenty minutes to Vail," the Sheriff said telling us more than we needed.

Shortly, Leland came out with a heavy coat and a big stocking cap on his head. He opened up the big barn door and exposed a large red gasoline tank. He filled a ten-gallon gas can. He then brought it over to our snowmobiles and using a funnel, he filled each of our tanks. After doing that he swished the gas can and I heard a small amount of gas still in the can. He turned to the Sheriff and said that will be twenty-five dollars. The Sheriff pulled out his wallet and gave Leland the money. He said as he did,

Rod Beach

"Leland, please give me a receipt so I can get my money back from the County."

Leland reached over to a cardboard box, tore off a flap and wrote out the Sheriff's receipt. I looked at Sidney and he was just shaking his head.

We then went back to Jaquan's Bar and Grill and had a large breakfast. I looked at my watch as we left and noticed it was already almost ten o'clock.

The Sheriff lead us back out of town and drove down a steep embankment to the old railroad tracks. He stopped on the snow that covered the tracks and motioned us to come up next to him. "This is the old railroad track to the mine. It was built in 1889 and was used until the mine was closed and flooded. As we go, the first site you will see is the magnificent green bridge that US-24 uses to spans the Eagle River canyon. It is only about two miles up to the processing plant but the tracks may have fallen rocks on them so we will have to be careful to drive around them. We will also go through a tunnel that also many have rocks on the tracks. Just follow me closely and I think we will be okay."

The Ghost of Gilman

Both Sidney and I gave him the okay sign with our gloved hands. We started down the tracks slowly making sure we stayed between the rails. It looked like there was at least two feet of snow on the lever. The tracks followed the river as it curved it's way through the canyon. High rock cliffs were on each side of the right side of the tracks and on the left side of the river.

The trip took much more time than I imagined. There's something peculiarly fun about driving on railroad tracks. AS we rounded one sharp curve, I saw a big black hole in the rocks immediately ahead of us. Then I realized that must be the tunnel. AS we entered, we could see the exit just a short distance ahead of us. We traveled another quarter mile before we saw in the distance a group of buildings along the canyon wall on the right. In addition to the loading facility that was used for loading mined materials onto train cars, there were processing facilities with huge rotating drums, a maze of rooms and floors with scads of heavy-duty equipment and an ungodly number of pipes and electrical wires, fuse boxes and gauges.

This is when I understood the real depth of the operations here. I realized how different places evoke different senses as the primary one, even though this was a "ghost town," completely silent save for the racket made by us on our snowmobiles. The noise when everything was simultaneously operational must have been stupendous. I stood and tried to imagine how it must have sounded with all the massive machinery, the pipes and gears and tracks and pumps, and a train whistle to boot. It must have been very loud.

I noticed the processing facility with it's tall tower was falling in on itself. The loading facility that sat on the south side of all of the numerous old buildings, was still standing although was badly weathered. I noticed as we approached the entire facility, the door to the loading facility was open. We stopped directly in front of the building and all got off. Not knowing what we would find, we approached the building slowly. I was the first to reach the front door and peered into the darkness inside. I noticed a strange smell. The Sheriff then entered holding a flashlight he had extracted from his back pack and started looking around.

The beam of light painted a swathe of light as it hit each wall. He then lowered the light to the floor and stopped when he saw something lying on the floor in the corner. Looking closely, I noticed there were two bodies laying flat on the floor with their hands clasped together. I assumed it was Bill and Wilma Wise.

The Sheriff stood silent as I approached the bodies. I reached down to see if I could detect a pulse and discovered as I picked up Bill's hand, it was cold and clammy. I dropped it immediately. Meanwhile, the Sheriff took his backpack off and reached into it extracting a small gas lantern. He pumped the pressure up and then lit the mantels. Soon the entire loading facility was full of light.

I noticed an old desk and file cabinet on the opposite end of the room as well as many other items that would be used to monitor the amount of ore being loaded. I walked back outside and on the south end of the facility was a large open top metal container that was just under a long conveyor system that brought the ore from the processing facility to the loading facility. Another conveyor that was now lying down on the ground would then take the ore from that

Rod Beach

large container over to the train tracks where empty ore cars would be loaded.

When I started back into the loading office, Sidney was coming out holding his SAT phone. I stood by him as he said, "Officer Jackson, we have two dead bodies here in the old mining town of Gilman. We need you to come up to Red Cliff today so we can have you look at this death scene and determine what happen and when. I think the road from Minturn to Red Cliff is now open so I would suggest you come that way. Let me know when you reach Minturn and I will ride my snowmobile back to Red Cliff and bring you to the scene. I think if you leave soon, it will take you about three or four hours. I-70 should be okay by now so try to get here as soon as possible. Cal and I will stay her with Sheriff Jameson of Eagle County and see if we can find any other clues on what may have happen to this man and his wife. Please hurry and dress warmly."

I guessed Officer Jackson would not delay since Sidney had made that call. When Sidney switched off his SAT phone, he turned to me and said, "We need to look around a little and see if we can find any clues or other evidence that can help Officer

75

The Ghost of Gilman

Jackson when he gets here. I don't want to move the bodies until he gets here so we don't disturb anything he may use to help us. Why don't we look around this area and the other building s and see if we can see any tracks or other evidence in the meantime."

Just then Sheriff came out of the old building and said, "I was down on my knees looking at the bodies when a rat crawled away from the woman's body. It ran back down a rat hole in the corner of the building. The entire place is full of rat droppings and that is why it smells so badly in addition to the smell of the rotting bodies. I think they may have been dead at least a week."

"Yes," I said. "I noticed the droppings as I tried to find Bill's pulse. His entire body was clammy, so I just released it. Our Forensics Expert is on his way, so we don't want to move the body. We are going to look around for any clues that may help us find out what happened here. The thing that I keep wondering is, how did those two old people get down here from the top of the mountain since the old wooden stairs are unusable. I think I will look for another trail. Joan told me her father would sometimes use another trail down to his loading facility. They may have used that trail."

"That is a good idea Cal. I'm going walk up to the end of these buildings and maybe I can find something to help us. Sheriff, why don't you walk behind these building and look for any foot prints or other evidence. We need to find out why these people died here. Were they killed or just lay down there to die from their diabetic conditions. We may have just a regular death situation here and not a violent crime," Sidney explained to both the Sheriff and me.

I went back to my snowmobile and extracted my binoculars out and started scanning the tall cliff to the top. After a few minutes, I saw a small trail about fifty-yards south of the loading facility that went up the steep hill. I went down and found the trail that was covered with about three inches of snow. I followed the trail up the hill about one-hundred yards when I encounter a large land slide of soft sand and soil. Since there was no snow on this area, I saw another small three-foot wide recent disturbance in the sandy soil. Using my binoculars, I followed this recent slide and discovered it ended at another small trail over the rocks that continued winding it's way to the top ending at the west end of Gilman where the Club House was located. I wondered if they decided to slide down the soft soil to the lower trail believing before the earth slide the trail probably went across it. I made a mental note to have Officer Jackson look for dirt on the body's back side since that would confirm how they got down.

Returning to the loading facility, I didn't see the Sheriff or Sidney. I decided to walk north and see if I could find them. During this walk, I was surprised to find the large processing facility that was falling into itself because of the rotting roof timbers. Since I didn't either Sidney or the Sheriff, I went back down to the loading facility. Just then, I heard Sidney calling me from the other side of the railroad tracks. I followed his voice and looked down on a second set of tracks that ran by a nice building. I went on down to that building and discovered it was a train station probably built much later than the other buildings. It was a well-built cement block structure that still had a number of benches for customers to wait for the train. As I walked into the lobby, I saw the Sheriff putting wood into an old wood burning stove.

Rod Beach

Sidney noticed me and said, "The Sheriff said this station was built by the railroad in about 1956 after the tracks were extended to Minturn. It will be a warmer place to wait for Officer Jackson. What did you find?"

I explained what I discovered and they both agreed with my opinion on how the couple came down the cliff.

Sidney turn to the Sheriff who had finished lighting the stove and said, "We call Cal the magic man since he always finds clues that help us solve crimes. When Officer Jackson arrives, he can see if the back sides of the corpses have soil on them so we can determine if his magic has help solve this part of the crime."

The Sheriff just nodded and said. "Well, by my mental calculations, your man won't be here before two o'clock, so we have at least a three hour wait. Do you want to wait here or just go back to Red Cliff?"

Sidney thought for a few moments and then said, "Well we have to go get Officer Jackson when he arrives so we might as well go back and relax for a while until he arrives. I will call him and tell him to meet us at the hotel."

The Ghost of Gilman

With that statement, we all got back onto our snowmobiles and headed back. When we were about half way back, the Sheriff's SAT phone started ringing. He stopped his snowmobile and retrieved his SAT phone. When he answered it, he listen for a few seconds and then said, "Can you send someone over to Red Cliff to pick me up. Have them bring a snowmobile trailer so I can bring my snowmobile back with me. I'll see you in about an hour."

He turned to us and said, "There has been a bad wreck in Eagle, so I have to return now. I'm sure you two can handle this situation without me now that you have found the bodies."

Sidney responded, "Yes, we understand. We will continue our investigation here and you take care of your problem in Eagle."

When we arrived back at the hotel, the Sheriff checked out and paid Alice with a County Check. We decided to check Officer Jackson into his room since he would most likely have to stay overnight here after he finished his examination.

About one-thirty in the afternoon, Officer Jackson pulled up in front of the hotel in another CBI Yukon. Sidney and I went out to meet him and Sidney asked, "How were the roads? You made very good time."

Officer Jackson answered, "The roads were all cleared so I was able to drive at the speed limit. Now, where are the bodies located?"

Sidney replied as he realized Officer Jackson was dressed in some warm coveralls, "It is about two miles down the canyon toward Minturn. We have to take snowmobiles since there is no road there. You can just climb behind me and we will start down the railroad tracks.

When we arrived, we took Officer Jackson into the loading facility. When he saw the two bodies, he rubbed his chin, held his nose and said, "These bodies have been here for over five or six days. They are starting to decompose. I need to get started. Do we have a light so I can see better."

I replied, "Sidney, do you think I should go get that gas light down at the train station?"

Sidney just nodded and I left quickly. When I returned, Officer Jackson had his back pack off and was laying different instruments and bottles of solutions out

The Ghost of Gilman

onto the desk. When I lighted the gas lamp, I saw for the first time how badly the bodies looked. Their skin was almost pure white with some blue spots on their faces around their mouth.

Sidney was telling Officer Jackson about my theory on how the couple had come down to the bottom of the canyon, so he needed to look at the back sides of each body.

Officer Jackson in his normal disgruntled tone of voice said, "Sir, don't start telling me what my job is. I will examine everything you need to know."

I looked at Sidney who just motioned me outside. He turned to Officer Jackson and said, "We will be in a much newer building across the tracks down by another set of tracks and the river. When you complete your investigation, please find us there."

Sidney and I left taking our backpacks with us. When we sat down on one of the high-backed railroad benches, he reached into his backpack and finally found a deck of cards. We may as well enjoy ourselves for a while since if I know Officer Jackson, we will be here the rest of the afternoon. So why don't we play some rummy?"

Rod Beach

"That is one thing I have never done before on any investigation, but it will help pass the time," I replied smiling.

We played for over two hours when Officer Jackson came into the train station. I have done everything I can do here. I need to get these bodies back to a laboratory where I can do more. Is there a laboratory around here?

I don't know but I'll make a couple of phone calls. I guess I should probably start with the Vail Police," He replied taking out his SAT phone.

He opened up a small black notebook containing pages of phone numbers and then dialed a number. When someone answered he said, "This is Sidney Kingsbury of the CBI. Can you put the Chief on the phone."

After a short pause, Sidney said, "Hello Chief, we have found the bodies of two elder man and wife in the loading facility at Gilman. My Forensics Expert needs to us a lab to perform some more research on what happen to these people. Do you have a forensics lab?"

Sidney listened to his response and then

said, "We have to get these bodies back to Red Cliff so if you could send an ambulance over there to pick them up, I would appreciate it. I think the road will now be open so I think you can now drive your ambulance or rescue unit here with no problem. In addition, we left the snow mobile trailers in Minturn so could you have someone pick them up and bring them to Red Cliff so we can return them to you."

"Yes, that would probably be a better choice, Sidney said after hearing the Chief's response.

He listened again and then said, "Yes, we have a CBI Yukon in Red Cliff so we can use it to get our other vehicle in Minturn so we only will need the ambulance now. We'll see you soon."

Chapter 6

Sidney turned to me and said, "We need to find something we can use to take these bodies back to Red Cliff. Let's look around and see if we can take some metal roofing material to use to lay the bodies on for the trip back."

I looked at him and said, "I noticed that the processing building had caved in and exposed metal roofing material. I think we can pry some of it off and use them."

"That will work. Let's go get some and make a sled for each of the bodies that we can pull behind the snowmobiles. We will have to go slowly but I think that may work."

The Ghost of Gilman

We found four sheets of metal roofing material about three feet wide and ten feet long. I also found some strong wire and twisted off about forty-feet of it. We wired two of the metal sheets together and then punch a hole in one end with an old nail. We put one end of the wire into the hole and twisted it tight. Then we stretched the wire out for about twenty feet and twisted and broke it off. We did the same thing for the other sled and when we had both sleds built, we went into the loading facility where Officer Jackson was putting his gear back into his backpack.

As we started to lift the woman up to carry her out to the sleds, we had built, Officer Jackson yelled, "Here put these rubber gloves on. These bodies may have all kinds of bacteria on them. You need to protect yourselves. In addition, I have found some finger prints on the man's body that I don't want to disturb them. Just pick them up by the arms where their cloths are since the prints are on the man's head."

We each put on the rubber gloves and gently carried each body out to the sleds and laid them gently down. Sidney took some rope out of his backpack and tied them down to each sled. After we had completed that task, Sidney got onto his snowmobile and motioned Officer Jackson to sit behind him. I climbed onto my snowmobile and we headed slowly to Red Cliff.

When we drove down the street toward the hotel, several people started following us. When we stopped, one woman came up to where the couple were lying on the sleds and started crying. "Oh no! Not Bill and Wilma. They were such good people."

We arrived about five minutes before the Vail Rescue Unit pulled up in front of the hotel. Two Medical Technicians got out and just undid the tow wire from the sleds and picked up the two bodies using the metal roofing sheets to carry then to their unit. They carefully slid them onto their floor and closed the door.

They turned to me and said. "The Chief said to park our snowmobiles behind the hotel, and he will have them picked up tomorrow. He also said, since you have your own transportation to Vail so we will take these bodies to our Forensics Lab you your man can perform a more extensive investigation. Is that right?"

The Ghost of Gilman

Sidney responded, "Yes that is right. We will drop Officer Jackson off at your lab and then we will go to Minturn to get our other vehicle. We will also bring the snowmobile trailer back to your office when we do, you won't have to worry about that duty."

"That sounds like a great plan," One of the men said as he climbed into his rescue vehicle.

Sidney and I checked out of the hotel and told Alice that we appreciated her place. Sidney then climbed into the Yukon Officer Jackson had driven and we headed back to Vail. The road was completely different than US-24 that we experienced on the snowmobile. To me It didn't seem to be as curvy and was downhill most of the way after we topped the mountain just northeast of Gilman.

We arrived in Vail after passing numerous ski slopes filled with skiers who were enjoying the deep powder snow. When we arrived at the Vail Police Station, Officer Jackson got out and in without saying anything to either Sidney or me. Sidney and I then headed back to Minturn. We picked up the Vail Police snowmobile trailer and headed back to Vail. On the way to Vail,

Rod Beach

Sidney started telling me what he though I should do next.

"I'm going to take this Yukon back to Denver tomorrow afternoon after Officer Jackson after he completes his examinations and determines the cause of death. I will also take him with me. If he determines they were murdered instead of just dying from complications of the diabetics, then you need to start investigating who could have killed them and why. Therefore, we will have to get three rooms in Vail for tonight if there are any available. I will have the Chief call to arrange rooms for us since he probably knows where they will be available."

Okay, that sounds good to me. I have already determined three persons who I would want to talk to about it if he declares it was a murder. There is Joe Sample, Andy Alverez, and Sam Wilcox. All of them have some kind of record that indicates they may be capable of murder," I responded.

"Yes, I agree with you, but let's wait for OJ's Report. He should be finished by tomorrow afternoon. Then you can use your hotel room in Vail for your investigation," Sidney instructed.

The Ghost of Gilman

As we pulled back into the Vail Police Station, we went in to talk with Chief Dunny.

As we entered, he had his secretary bring us two cups of coffee. He then said, "It sounds like you had quite a trip up the Eagle Canyon. How deep was the snow up on the top?"

Sidney smiled as he took a sip of coffee and replied, "It was really deep going up through the trees before the big switch back but on top the wind blew most of it off. It was only about two feet deep there. However down along the railroad tracks in Eagle Canyon, it was again about three or four feet deep. Your snowmobiles worked great, Thank you helping us with those. I don't know how we would have managed without them. They are even fun to ride."

"Yes, I enjoy snowmobiling as well. Sometimes I spend several days traveling over many of the high mountains around here on the snowmobile," the Chief replied.

Sidney changed the subject and asked, "Chief, do you have a recommendation where we can get a room for the night here in Vail?"

Rod Beach

"Yes, there are several places that offer us a special rate so let me have my secretary make some calls," he said as he picked up his phone. "Sally, can you find three rooms for tonight for our CBI visitors from Denver?"

After a few seconds he hung up the phone and said, "Sally will find you three rooms. You know the town is nearly full since there is so much powder on the slopes now."

"Yes, I told Cal that may be the case. We saw people all over the slopes on our way from Red Cliff this afternoon," Sidney responded finishing his coffee.

"What are your plans for this afternoon and evening?" the Chief asked.

"Well, our Officer Jackson will be busy tonight and probably will finish tomorrow morning so he and I will return to Denver. However, if he determines the two were murdered, then Detective York will stay here and try to find the person or persons responsible. He is one of my best detectives and has been very successful solving difficult cases," Sidney said.

"Yes, I have followed his career for a number of years now. I wish I had someone like him working for me," the Chief said.

"Don't get any ideas, Dunny," Sidney said with a strong voice. "I lost another good detective recently who left for more money. I wouldn't want to lose Cal."

"Don't worry Sidney. My budget can't afford another highly paid man at this time," the Chief said trying to reduce Sidney's concern. "Now the reason I asked about your plans for tonight, I thought we could catch a good dinner. I'm sure my budget could afford that since I would be entertaining the CBI."

"Well that would be nice. Last night we ate in Jaquan's Bar and Grill. It was a great hamburger, but I would rather eat something like a steak or something," Sidney said.

"Well when Sally finds you a room, we can then make reservations for a nice dinner. My wife is visiting her parents in Salt Lake so I would like something besides a can of soup that I know how to fix," the Chief said laughing.

Just then Sally came into the Chief's office and said, "I have reserved three rooms at the Moose Head Lodge in Vail at our discount.

Who should I give them the names of the people staying overnight?"

Sidney answered quickly. "The names are Sidney Kingsbury, Calvin York, and Willard Jackson."

"Okay I will tell them that," she said.

Chief Dunny said good work Sally. That is an excellent hotel with a fine restaurant. Would you also make reservations at the restaurant for four at seven tonight in my name?"

"Okay Chief. I will let them know," Sally responded as she smile at us and left the office.

"Well, that's done. I need to get back to work, so you two go ahead and check in. I'll see you at seven."

We stood up and Sidney asked, "Where is your forensics lab?" Sidney asked. "We need to tell Officer Jackson where we will be and find out how he is doing."

"Just go back out to the reception desk and Sally will take you out to our lab that is located behind the Police Station," the Chief said as he stood to shake our hands.

The Ghost of Gilman

We finally found the lab and saw Officer Jackson working over one of the bodies. He never looked up from what he was doing and just motioned us to leave him alone. Sidney said, "When you are ready, give me a call and I will come and pick you up. We have three rooms at the Moose Head Lodge for tonight and the Chief is taking us to dinner at seven so you should plan to quite before that time. You can finish tomorrow morning if you have too."

Officer Jackson just nodded and continued to do what he was doing. We just turned around and left to check into our rooms at the hotel.

The room was a very nice large room complete with a fireplace in the wall. It was furnished with pictures of mountain scenes. It even had a king bed. I thought the Chief must have a great discount to afford this kind of room. As I sat in a large comfortable chair, I called Mary to let her know what I was doing in Vail and what my plans were as of right now. I asked about the kids and told her I missed her and hoped to be home soon. I had just hung up the phone when I heard a knock on my door. When I opened the door, Sidney walked in.

Rod Beach

"Do you believe this room. Mine is almost the same and I really like the fireplace," Sidney said with an enthusiastic voice. "Now, I came by to tell you Officer Jackson called and he is ready to quit for the night. I'm going over to the Police Station and pick him up. When we get back, I will bring him here so he can brief us on what he had discovered so far. I'll see you soon."

About twenty minutes later, I heard another knock on my door. When I answered it, Sidney and Officer Jackson walked in and sat down on my two side chairs. I sat down on the edge of the bed as Officer Jackson started talking. "I have made a list of my preliminary finding so far:

> 1. The man's pockets were empty. No keys, no ID, no billfold, not even a handkerchief.
> 2. He didn't find the woman's purse so she must have left it in their car.
> 3. I checked their blood at the sight and found it not to contain too much sugar, so they didn't die of a lack of insulin.

The Ghost of Gilman

4. I could not find any wounds or blood on their clothes or any wound site.

5. When I examined both of their hairlines, their hair came out easily meaning they had been dead for some time.

6. When I got them back to the lab, I cut their clothes off and found a large amount of sandy soil so Cal's version of how they were able to get down to the bottom was right. I still didn't find any blood or even any wounds from a bullet or a knife, however both of them had a small hole in their chest that had just a small amount of blood on the skin.

7. I started opening the man's body and never found anything that may have killed him. I checked his stomach and didn't find any poison or undigested material. When I opened his chest cavity, it was full of blood and his heart had a fairly small puncture hole in it.

8. I found the same evidence on the woman's body.

9. I also found some places on their arms and legs where some animal had probably decided it would be good to eat. There were also a number of insects in the areas where they had been nibbling. I used some of these to establish the time of death.

10. I looked under their fingernails to see if there was any foreign substances but found none.

11 Now tomorrow, I want to test their body fluids that remains for any signs of poison but I'm not expecting any.

12 Tomorrow, I am going to x-ray their bodies to see if any of their bones may have splintered, broken, or had perforated their heats.

13 I should complete my tests and examination and will take the necessary pictures for my written report so you can both have it before I leave.

14 I have also found two sets of fingerprints on the body. One set on the head and neck of the

man and the other set on the face of the woman. I will be inserting them into our data base for a complete identification of who handled them after they were dead."

"There are some interesting items in your list Officer Jackson that will help Cal determine what he needs to do next," Sidney said. "If you find anything else tomorrow be sure you brief Cal before we leave for Denver."

I said, "Yes, I am very concerned about the keys to the car. The first thing I need to do is to stop by his car and look into it to see if there are any clues as to what happened to them. I also think you solved the problem about how the couple got down to the bottom of the mine. I only have one question, could they have been injured sliding down that soft sandy landslide?"

Officer Jackson considered my question before he answered. "No, if they had been injured, they would have had a hard time getting down into the building where we found them, but the x-rays will tell me more about that possibility. I plan on x-raying both bodies tomorrow morning to look for any broken bones in addition to try to determine the time of death. That will be a big problem since they are already starting to decompose but I know some new techniques that will help with that task."

I asked, "We need to determine the time of death. Will you be able to do determine that time?"

"Yes," he replied in his normal manner of trying to educate Sidney and me. "Decomposition begins almost instantly from the moment of death. As the heart stops beating, the body's cells are deprived of oxygen and pH changes occur. Cells gradually lose their structural integrity and begin to break down, releasing cellular enzymes which break down cells and tissues in a process known as autolysis, degraded by the body's own enzymes. There will be no obvious signs of decomposition, however internally bacteria within the gastrointestinal tract begin to digest the soft tissues of the organs. Throughout this stage certain early post-mortem indicators may begin to occur, such as livor mortis (pooling of blood in the body), rigor mortis (stiffening of muscles) and algor mortis (body temperature reduction). Between 2 to 6 days after death decomposition includes the first visible signs of decay, namely the inflation of the abdomen due to a build-up of various gases produced by bacteria inside the cadaver. This bloating is particularly visible around the tongue and eyes as the build-up of gases cause them to protrude. The skin may exhibit a certain color change, taking on a marbled appearance due to the transformation of hemoglobin in the blood into other pigments. Blood bubbles may form at the nostrils and other orifices. At this point an odor of putrefaction may be noticeable. Then between five to eleven days, the previously inflated carcass now deflates, and putrid internal gases are released. As the tissues break down the corpse will appear wet and strong odors are very noticeable. Various compounds contribute to the potent odor of a decomposing body, including cadaverine, putrescine, skatole, indole, and a variety of sulfur-containing compounds. Although foul-smelling to most, these putrid compounds will attract a range of insects and other animals like the rats we found. Fluids begin to drain from the corpse via any available orifice, particularly the nose and mouth. The internal organs typically decompose in a particular order, starting with the intestines and ending with the prostate or uterus. Then between ten to twenty-four days, the body, decomposition slows, as most of the flesh has been stripped from the skeleton, though some may remain in denser areas such as the abdomen. The previously strong odors of decay begin to subside, though a cheese-like smell may persist caused by butyric acid. If the body has decayed on soil, the area around the cadaver may show signs of plant death. Even though the bodies were laying on an old wooden floor, I saw some signs of butyric acid on the floor. So therefore, I put the time of death at no earlier than ten days, but the amount of butyric acid was not enough to be more than eleven days. I put down the time of death as ten days before you found the body."

"Okay, we found the body on Tuesday of this week and you examined the body on Wednesday, so the deaths most likely occurred on the previous Monday or Tuesday. Is that right?"

"Yes," he said. "I would agree with that date." Officer Jackson said. "In fact, I put that date down as the time of death in my report."

The Ghost of Gilman

"One last question," I said, "Did you take fingerprints of the people we arrested?"

"Yes, and I have sent them into the National Finger Print Data Base, and they indicated by tomorrow, they will have everything we would need to identify them as the killers>"

I made a note in my notebook of this date and looked at Sidney who said, "Okay Cal you can do your magic."

After the briefing we went down to the restaurant to meet the Chief and had a delicious dinner of prime rib with all the trimmings.

Chapter 7

Early the next morning, I drove back toward Red Cliff and stopped at the Gilman Gate to check Bill's Car to see if he left his keys and billfold in it. As I got to the road leading into Gilman Gate, I was astonished the car was missing. I saw in the deep snow where it had backed away from the gate, turned around and earlier in the morning. I now knew someone had the keys and had stolen the car.

I continued on down to Red Cliff and checked back into the hotel. I asked Alice, "Did you see Bill and Wilma's car in Red Cliff this morning?

The Ghost of Gilman

"Yes, I did. It was driving up toward their house, but I didn't see who was driving it. You may find it up at their house."

I immediately jumped back into my Yukon and headed up to their house. When I got there, I went in and found that someone had cleaned out the spare bedroom. I looked around and didn't find anything else that would help me. I wondered, if Sam Wilcox had killed Bill and Wilma so my first thought was to put out an APB for the 1967 Chevrolet.

I called Sidney on my SAT phone and told him what I had discovered. I said, "Could you have Chief Dunny put out an APB for a 1967 Chevrolet with Colorado plates. and asked him to have the Chief put out the APB."

Sidney replied, "What color is the old car?"

I said, "I don't know but I think I can find out. I will call you back in a few minutes with that information."

I wondered how I could find what color the old car was and then remembered something Alice had told us earlier.

I decided to stop by Jaquan's Bar and Grill

and see if they were there having coffee with their normal coffee buddies.

When I walked in, I noticed about ten or twelve men sitting at a long table in the front of the bar. I walked up and sat down at one end of the table. Jaquan brought me big cup of coffee and turned to the others at the table and said, "Guys, this is a CBI detective who is trying to find Bill and his wife. He may want to talk with you about what he needs. Help him if you can."

I thanked Jaquan for his introduction to the group and I stood and said, "I no longer am searching for Bill and his wife. I found them yesterday morning lying dead in the loading facility at the old Gilman mine. Someone had killed them. I am now looking for who may have done that deed."

"Is that why the rescue unit from Vail was here yesterday?" One old timer asked.

"Yes, we took the two bodies to the Vail Police station so we could perform a more detailed examination of the bodies," I explained.

"Most of the old timers were surprised with my news. One asked, "Do you have any idea who may have killed them?"

The Ghost of Gilman

"I have a number, but I also have just discovered that someone stole Bill's old 1967 Chevrolet. Do any of you know what color the car was? I asked.

Another older man replied, "Yes, Bill always said it was Salman and Grey. It was a very nice old car that he really loved."

"Good, I need to make a quick call back to Vail. Excuse me while I make that call and then I need some more information from you," I said as I pulled out my SAT phone and called Sidney and gave him the color.

When I finished, I shut off my SAT phone and one old timer said, "That is the strangest cell phone I have ever seen. What kind is it?"

"This is a satellite phone. I can call anyone from the deepest canyon or highest mountain using a satellite that is flying overhead. I do not have to rely on the various cell towers. It comes in handy when I am working in remote areas," I replied to the group of old men.

One man looked at the others and said, "How about that. I think I will get one since my cell phone doesn't work when I'm up at my cabin. I wonder what they will think of next!"

Rod Beach

I ignored that comment and asked, "Does Bill usually leave his keys in his car when he is away from it?"

"No, there usually isn't any need to carry your keys up here. Everybody knows everybody else," another old man said.

"Well has anyone seen Bill's car in town today?" I asked.

Everyone looked at each other and finally one man said, "We have been in here since eight o'clock this morning. I was wondering where Bill was since he hasn't been here for the past week or ten days. I just thought they may be visiting their daughter in Denver or their son in Colorado Springs. Now you tell us that someone may have killed him for his car?"

"I'm not sure that was the reasons, but I do have to consider that as a possible motive. That car is probably fairly expensive if it was in good shape," I replied. "Now, another question. Have anyone of you seen Sam Wilcox lately?"

Again, they looked at each other and then another man at the end of the table said, "I don't know if Sam is still in Red Cliff. I usually see him working around town doing different chores, but I haven't seen him for over two weeks. Do you think he may be involved?"

"Right now, I have no other suspects. I plan to be in Red Cliff for a few days so if anyone sees Sam, please let me know. I'm staying at the hotel for a while. Do any of you know if Bill had any trouble with anyone else?"

All the men started talking about different people in town and finally one said, "I don't know if Bill even knew Joe Sample, but I saw him in town last week. Joe has been in a lot of trouble in a number of places around the county and I didn't know what he was doing in Red Cliff. I didn't see him do anything illegal, but I always wondered about him."

Most of the other men agreed with this man. I said, "I'm going to give you the number to this SAT phone so if any of you see something that could help me find this killer, please give me a call.

I wrote the number down on a small piece of paper Jaquan provided me and handed it to each of the old men. "I want to thank you for your information. It has been good having coffee with you this morning. Do you think I could come again tomorrow morning? That way if any of you hear anything you can tell me while we drink some of this good coffee."

They all agreed they would welcome me to their group, and I left.

I then went back to the hotel to talk with Alice and let her know about Bill and Wilma. When I walked in, she was sitting on a high stool behind the counter. She looked up and asked, "Is the Sheriff with you Detective York?

"No," I replied. "He had a problem he had to solve in Eagle. I am now here by myself since my boss and our Forensics Expert are heading back to Denver this afternoon. I have to find out who killed Bill and Wilma."

"Oh, you think they were killed. Most folks around here thought they probably just went up to the old mind, laid down, and died. How did they die anyway?" she finally asked.

I won't know until later this afternoon but I'm sure they just did not lay down and die<" I said. "Now what room can you put me into for a couple of days?"

"I don't have too many people here right now

so, you can have the corner room that looks out on Main Street. If you are still here by Friday night, I may have to move you since there is a big shot from Denver who has reserved that room since he and his girlfriend are skiing next weekend," she said.

"Ok, I can live with that," I replied. "Right now, I have to go up to my room and call my wife."

She handed me the keys to the corner room, and I went in. I immediately saw why the man from Denver wanted this room. It was much larger that the previous room I had there and was much nicer furnished. I sat down in a big chair, looked up main street toward the high mountains to the east, and dialed Mary's number at the State Capitol. When she answered, I said, "Hey honey, I have a little time right now so I thought I would give you a call. I hope everything is going well at home."

Mary laughed replying, "Yes, everything is going well. The kids miss their daddy and I miss you too, but we hope you will be home soon. How is it going today."

I explained everything that was happening and what I was planning on doing next. As

Rod Beach

I was talking. I realized, I had not called Joan Ault about the death of her parents. I quickly wrote Joan down on a notepad on the table. Mary continued telling me about the different things the kids were doing, what she was doing, and that the snow in Denver was almost gone.

After about five minutes, I said, "Honey, I have to make another call, so I need to hang up now. I will try to call you later today or early tomorrow. Bye!"

I switched off the SAT phone, looked up Joan's number and punched it into the phone. After three rings, I heard her on the other end say, "Hello, this is Joan Ault. Who is calling?"

I realized she would not recognize my Sat phone number, so I quickly said, "Joan, this is Calvin York and I'm calling from Red Cliff on my SAT phone."

"Oh, hi Detective York. I'm glad to hear your voice. Did you find my parents yet?"

"Yes, we did. We found both of them in the loading facility at the Gilman mine. Unfortunately, both of them were dead. I'm sorry to be so blunt, but I didn't know how else to tell you."

She replied with a resolute voice, "I expected as much. Since they had not called either me or my brother, I expected something had happened to them. Did they have a diabetic episode?"

"No, it looks like someone killed them," I said. "We found their car at the gate to Gilman and searched all over the old town but didn't find any trace of them. Of course, two to three feet of snow probably covered up any evidence anyway. We then decided to look at the building at the bottom of the mine and had to go back through Red Cliff and down the railroad tracks and we finally found them lying on the floor of the old loading facility. They had been there for at least a week. We were able to remove them, and they are now at the Vail Police Forensics Laboratory. I hope to hear this afternoon exactly how they did die but it looks to me to be a murder. Do you know anyone who may have had a disagreement with either of them?"

"No, I don't know too many people up there anymore, but I will put my thinking cap on and see if I can come up with something.

Rod Beach

Will you be in Red Cliff for a couple more days?"

"Yes, and the best way to get in touch with me is on this number. Do you have it on your cell phone?" I said.

"Yes, I have it. I will think about different people they knew and if I come up with anything, I will call you. Okay?"

"Yes, I would appreciate any help you can give me.

I looked at my watch and saw that it was now twelve-thirty, so I decided to go get a hamburger at Jaquan's. Just as I was leaving the hotel, my SAT phone range. I was Officer Jackson who indicated, they had indeed been stabbed with something long, thin, and sharp. He said he thought it may have been an ice pick or a long type of needle. He further indicated, he put the cause of death as a murder.

I went on down to Jaquan's and had a burger and fries and then tried to determine what I needed to do next.

I took a chance thinking the man who stole Bill's car may have needed some fuel, so I went to talk with Leland to see if anyone purchased any gasoline from him this morning. When I arrived, he answered his door with his normal sour mood. I showed him my badge and asked, "Did anyone buy any gasoline from you this morning?"

"Yes, Andy Alverez came by with a five gallon can and said someone had ran out of gas just north of town and he said he was bringing him some so he could get to Minturn."

"Was Andy driving an old Chevrolet?" I asked.

"No, he was in his old red pickup truck. He just placed the five gallon can in the back of his truck and headed out of town."

"How long ago was that?" I asked.

Leland replied, It probably was about ten minutes ago."

I got back into my Yukon and headed north on US-24 thinking I may be able to find either Andy or Bill's car. I drove as fast as I could and when, I saw Andy turning around at County Road 709, I stopped and asked, "Did you just put some gasoline into an old Chevrolet?"

Rod Beach

"Yes, Sam Wilcox was driving old Bill Wise's car and had ran out of gas. I brought him some and he just left. He said he was going to Minturn to buy some groceries for Bill and Wilma?"

I thanked him and headed to Minturn at a high rate of speed. When I drove into the outskirts of Minturn, I spotted Bill's old car at the first filling station on the road. I pulled into the station and parked next to the old Chevrolet, jumped out and waited until I saw a man come out after paying for the gasoline.

When he approached the car, I walked up to him with my badge showing and said, "Sam, you are under arrest for the murder of William and Wilma Wise. Put your hands behind your back and let me cuff you."

Sam looked at me and said, "What do you mean. Bill and Wilma were killed. I didn't know that. I saw Bill's car at the gate to Gilman this morning and thought they must have caught a ride home, so I just returned to the house. I knew Bill didn't like the mess in my room, so I cleaned it all out and decided to come to Minturn to find them. I checked around Red Cliff last night and they were not there so I figured they must be in

Minturn. I am just bringing their car back to them here."

"I'm sorry, I don't believe that story Sam," I said, "I'm taking you to jail in Eagle to stand trial for the murder of Bill and Wilma. "Now turn around so I can cuff you."

He turned around and I cuffed him. I put him into the back seat of the Yukon and secured each of his hands to the arm rests on each side of the vehicle. I then went into the filling station and asked if I could park the old Chevrolet there for a day or two. The owner said I could so I pulled it in next to the north end of the station out of the way of any doors the station may have to use.

I then took Sam to Eagle and up to the County Jail. I deposited him into the jail and then went to see Sheriff Jameson and told him what had happened.

Sheriff Jameson looked at me with a surprised look on his face, "Are you sure you have the right man?"

Our Forensics Officer indicated he obtained some finger prints from the body and we need to check those against Sam's finger prints. Can you have someone take Sam's for me to sent back to Denver just to make sure."

"Yes, I will have our Deputies do that right now," the Sheriff answered.

After about twenty minutes, a Deputy came in with ink prints from Sam Wilcox. I used the Sheriff's computer and sent them down to Officer Jackson with directions to check these prints with the ones he had from the bodies and then to get back to me as soon as possible.

I waited patiently for about an hour hoping the prints matched. When my SAT phone range, I answered it. "This is Detective Calvin York."

Officer Jackson started talking, "Cal, the prints do not match. You have arrested the wrong person. You need to release him as soon as possible. We don't need to fight a false arrest case right now."

I was astonished. "Okay, I understand, I will take him back to Minturn."

I turned to Sheriff Jameson and told him what we had to do. He ordered the deputies to bring him into his office. When they arrived, he didn't have any handcuffs on him. I stood and faced him and said, "I'm sorry Sam for thinking you killed Bill and Wilma. I hope you understand. I do however need your help in solving this case. You know both of these people well since you lived with them. I believe, their children will let you stay in their house for now and even let you drive their car. I will make that suggestion to them if you agree to help me."

Sam smiled and said, "I understand how you could have made this mistake. As I was sitting in jail, I started thinking about why their car was at the gate for almost a week. They told me they were going to go up to Gilman to celebrate their fifty years of marriage, and I just figured they must have walked back home for some reason. Their car were almost out of gas when I found it car."

I said, "I'm sorry I arrested you before I got all the facts. Can you help me find the real killer?"

Sam thought about my question with a frown on his face. Finally, he said, "I think someone probably needed some gas so they siphoned some out of their tank. I was drove their car to Minturn since I knew they had some friends here and maybe they were here. Anyway, I will do what ever you want to help you find the real killer."

"Thank you, Sam. I appreciate that. Now let's go back and get their car so we can start looking for the real killer," I said.

The Ghost of Gilman

Chapter 8

I drove Sam back to Minturn and we picked up Bill's car. I followed Sam back to Bill and Wilma's house and he parked the car in the garage and closed the door.

We then went into the house. Sam took me into the couple's bedroom where he had put most of his belongings and I helped him carry everything back into the spare bedroom. I thought to myself, I should have looked in the other bedroom before I jumped to the conclusion I did.

I then showed Sam the two notes I had found. "Who do you think this Andy is?"

The Ghost of Gilman

"The only Andy I know is Andy Alverez. I have no idea why Bill would write that note. I guess we should talk with Andy and see what he has to say," Sam replied nervously.

"What about the note he wrote that he wanted to talk with you about Joe Sample. Do you know what that is all about?" I asked.

"Again, I don't know. He never mentioned that to me. I happen to know Joe Sample. He is a bad apple. He is in jail more than he is out of jail. It seems like Sheriff Jameson has a grudge against him since he is always putting Joe in jail. I know he is not there now since I didn't see anyone else when you jailed me," Sam said smiling. "Maybe you should talk with their two children. They may know something about Joe Sample."

I thought about what he was saying. "You know, I talked with their daughter just this morning to let her know about her parents. I guess I should also call her brother. Do you know his phone number?"

"No, but I know where Wilma kept her phone book. I will go and get it," he replied.

A short time later he returned and handed me the small black notebook with a lot of phone numbers in it. There on the first page was the numbers of both Joan and Albert. I used their phone and called the number in the book for Albert.

The phone rang several times and finally a man answered, Hello, this is Al Wise, can I help you?"

"Yes, I hope you can. My name is Detective Calvin York of the CBI and I'm calling you from your parent's house. I'm sure you know by now, they both were killed up in the old Ghost Town of Gilman. I am investigating this crime and I'm presently in Red Cliff. I would like to ask you few questions. Do you have time right now?" I said.

"Yes, Joan called me this morning and told me about their deaths, but she didn't know many of the details. Can you fill me in of how they died?"

"Yes, from what I have found out right now is they went up to Gilman to celebrate their fifty years of married life. While there someone killed them and put them into the old loading facility where your father was the former foreman. We didn't find them for over ten days after they had been killed. They are both currently being stored in a cold room in Vail. I am trying to find out who may have killed them," I told him as much as I knew at the time.

"How were they killed?" He asked.

"They were basically killed with a long thin object like an ice pick that punctured their hearts. They probably died slowly. I'm sorry, but I need to ask you some questions. Do you have any idea who may have wanted them dead?"

"I have been away from that area for over fifteen years. I don't know any of their friends anymore or anyone who would want to kill them. They never caused anyone any problems," he said.

"I have found a note your father wrote to ask their border if he knew anything about a man called Joe Sample. Do you know Joe Sample?" I inquired.

"Yes, I know Joe. I have represented him a number of times in court. He is always getting in trouble. He may be a person you might want to talk with. I don't know if he is around anymore. The last time I represented him he said he was going to go to a warmer climate. I suggested that may be a good idea. I went to high school with Joe. We even played football and basketball together on the Battle Mountain High School teams. Therefore, he always calls me when he is in trouble to try to keep him out of jail. Sometimes it is difficult, but I have always been able to accomplish that feat. If he did kill dad and mom, I'm sorry I was so successful," he said with a sad voice.

"Do you know where I can find Joe now?" I inquired.

"I have no idea. I heard he didn't leave the area. I would guess he probably lives in Minturn or even Vail since that is where all the action is. Red Cliff is way too tame for him," he added.

"Well, I will try to find him and see what he has to say. If he did this killing, I would not think you should represent him. Now, do you know anyone else that your father or mother talked about that we should talk with?" I asked.

"That town is full of people who are trying to

The Ghost of Gilman

hide something in their past. If I were you, I would keep an open mind on everyone you talk with. I know the CBI has the capability to do extensive research on people, I would suggest you put some names into your data base search engine and see what comes out," he said.

I thought he had a good idea so I thanked him and said, "If you think of anything that can help me, please give me a call. You can get my SAT phone number from the CBI since that is the best way to get me where ever I'm at in these mountains,"

"Alright, let me think about what you have told me and if I come up with something, I will call you. Good luck on your investigation."

I sat down with Sam and we created a list of names that I wanted information on before I called Ben Hamilton, the CBI Data Base Manager.

Sam started naming names. "I think you should include Jaquan the owner of the bar and grill since he was an unknown person before he came here. You also should also include Alice Wilson although she has been here forever, she may have something in her background that Bill or Wilma discovered. Then there is Leland Harvey, the man who sells gasoline. He treated me very bad this morning for some reason. I also know you mentioned Andy Alverez. I have never met him but obviously Bill has since his note indicated he needed to call him. There are a number of old men who Bill always had coffee with that may have a grudge with Bill since most of them were old miners years ago. I guess I wouldn't exclude the Sheriff and his deputies since they run this county like a country club. Maybe you should get the names of people who were here at the time Bill and Wilma went up to Gilman. There may be someone who was here at the time that had some long festering grudge against Bill. How many names do you want to start with?"

"Well, you have mentioned way too many, but I like the idea of people who were here at the hotel ten days ago. I never thought about that possibility. Thanks Sam. You already have helped me. I think I should go over to the hotel and get those names. I want you to stay here since I don't want people to think you are helping me. You may discretely asked people around town about what happen to Bill and Wilma. They may talk more with you than they would with me. I get the same feeling with some of the men at the morning coffee clutch. You just walk around town expressing your dismay with their deaths. Is that okay with you?"

I looked at my watch and was surprised it was almost five o'clock. Where did this day go? I went back to the hotel and walked up to the counter where Alice was busy working on a cross-word puzzle. When she saw me, she said, "Hey Detective York, how did your day go? Word is you arrested Sam Wilcox. Did he kill Bill and Wilma. I never trusted him ever since me came here."

"Yes, I did arrest him down in Minturn, but I discovered he didn't kill Bill and Wilma, so I brought him back to their house. On the way back here, I got to thinking that maybe someone who was staying here during that time may have had a grudge against Bill so I would like to see your appointment books for those days before and after they were killed. Can you get me that information?"

"I consider that private information," she replied.

"Well, if I have to get a warrant to see those

files I can so you may just as well let me see them now," I said forcefully

"Okay, here is my room assignments. You can look at anything I have but I hope you handle them discretely. If my guests find out that their information is open, then they will stop coming here," she said.

She handed me a large book of people in each of the rooms for the last three weeks. I said, I will look at this tonight and return it to you tomorrow morning. Is that alright with you?"

"Yes, I'm not expecting anyone to come in tonight so that would be fine," responded as she left the counter and went into her quarters.

I took the book up to my room and put it under my mattress until I returned from Jaquan's. I then walked out of the hotel and down the street to get a bite to eat. I had a couple of beers with my hamburger and while I was there, I talked with Jaquan and asked him where he came from.

Jaquan said, "I used to live in Bisbee, Arizona where my father work the mines down there. I really enjoyed this little town in the mountains when I visited his grandfather who worked at the mine up here. I had a small café down in Bisbee but when the mine closed, I decided to come up here and start this place."

"I spent some time in Bisbee. What is your father's name," I asked thinking I needed his last name for my list.

"You may have seen him around town. He still lives there but he is retired thanks to the United Mine Workers with their nice retirement policy. His name is Jaquan Alvarez."

I thought, that was a coincidence since that was the same name of Andy Alverez.

I then returned to my room. I saw someone had been in my room since I always left a few signs that would indicate someone had been looking for something. I wondered if Alice had second thoughts. I checked under the mattress and discovered the book was still there.

I sat down and started looking at the people who were in the hotel from twelve days ago until about last Monday. When I came to the page eleven days ago, I started writing down names. There were only fifteen people staying there that night. Most of these people were from Denver and Fort Collins and were probably skiers. Then I looked at the people who were there ten days ago and was surprised, according to the records, ten of the people from the night before stayed that night as well. However, two names stuck out when I saw then. One was Joe Sample and the other was Sheriff Jameson. I made a note of both of these names. Most of the other names were from out of town as far away as Texas and Ohio.

I thought I should have Ben check out these two names along with some that Sam had included. I listed in addition to Joe and the Sheriff, Leland Harvey, Andy Alvarez, and Jaquan Alvarez.

I called Ben and when he answered, I said, "Hey Ben, I need some information. I need you to run your quick data base and get me some information on several people up here in the mountains."

Ben replied, "Hey I wondered if you retired. You haven't asked me for any information for over a couple of months, but Sidney said you were in the mountains on another case. Who do you want me to run down."

"I need you to look into your data base for a quick answer for Andy Alverez, Jaquan Alverez, Leland Harvey, Alice Wilson, Joe Sample, and Sheriff Jameson. I need that information as soon as possible and then maybe a more thorough data search tonight. How long will it take to get me some early information on each of these people?"

"Okay, I have the names. However, do you have the first name for the Sheriff?" Ben inquired.

"No, I always just call him Sheriff. You can probably look it up. He is the Sheriff of Eagle County, Colorado. I don't know if he is involved but he may be, so I want the info on him as well," I replied.

"I can run their names through my top-level data and get you that information in about two hours. Then tonight I will run a more detailed data dump on each of them and I will get back to you tomorrow morning. Is that okay?"

"Yes, that will be great," I replied. "I'm going to give Sidney a call right now and brief him on what I have been doing up here in God's country. I will be available when you call me back."

I sat back and thought about what my next move would be. I thought I should go into Minturn after Ben calls me and check if Andy Alvarez or Joe Sample is there. I could drive over there and have a real dinner instead of another hamburger. I could check out the bars and talk with the Deputy while I am there to see if he has seen either of them lately.

I decided to call Sidney. When answered his phone, I asked, "How was your trip home?

"It was very quiet. I don't think Officer Jackson said more than three words to me all the way home. You have traveled with him. You know how talkative he gets.

"Yes, I discovered he doesn't like country music, so he always tells me to change the station. That's about all I can ever get out of him," I replied laughing.

"Well, have you made an arrest yet?" Sidney asked.

"No, but I have discovered a number of different suspects. I discovered, Jaquan's brother is Andy Alverez. I am trying to find him tonight in Minturn. I'm also going to try to find Joe Sample. I discovered Andy drives an old red pickup so I'm going to look for it tonight at some of the bars in Minturn."

"That's a good idea Cal. Just be careful if you find him. If he is the killer, he may not hesitate to kill again," Sidney cautioned me.

"I will," I said. "The other thing you should know, I arrested Sam Wilcox, but I discovered his fingerprints do not match those Officer Jackson found on the body, so I brought him back to the Wise house. He is now helping me find the killer. He suggested I look at the reservations at the hotel for ten and eleven days ago. When I did, I found out that Sheriff Jameson spent the night there as well as Joe Sample. I thought that was unusual so I'm going to follow up on that as well. I'm having Sam join the old men at their coffee each morning and listen to their ideas who may have killed Bill and his wife."

"Another good idea. Now, back to the Sheriff. It wouldn't be the first time a law officer became involved in a crime. Just make sure you have all the evidence in hand if you have to arrest him."

Rod Beach

"Yes, I know Sidney," I responded. "I am also having Ben run a quick data dump on a number of different people up here and he said he would call me soon. Then overnight, he is going to run a more detailed deep dump and get back to me tomorrow morning on these people. I have always discovered some interesting information from those deep dives into the background of the different suspects."

"I know," Sidney said. "Ben's ability has helped you a lot in the past. Let's hope he finds something interesting this time. Well, I have a meeting with the Director so I must be going. Keep in touch and good luck."

I had just switched off my SAT phone when it rang again. When I picked it up, I heard Ben's excited voice. "Cal, I think you have uncovered a big nest of criminals up there in Red Cliff. Are you sitting down?"

"Yes, I am sitting on my king-size bed right now. What have you discovered?" I asked.

"Well, there has been a rash of robberies in Eagle County. Some gang has been robbing a number of truck stops along I-70. So far, they have robbed six. On the first one in

The Ghost of Gilman

Gypsum, a camera was able to identify Joe Sample and Andy Alverez. The other five that occurred in Eagle, Walcott, Edwards, Vail, and Minturn, the two robbers had ski masks on but the size of them still makes them look like Joe and Andy. The last robbery occurred just three weeks ago in Minturn on a Tuesday night. The total take from these robberies exceed Fifteen-Thousand dollars. All of these robberies were investigated by Sheriff Jameson however, he has not made much headway if finding the culprits. The other thing that I found interesting is that Sheriff Jameson made a large Five-Thousand-dollar deposit into his bank account in Eagle."

"Wow! Do you think the Sheriff may be part of the gang involved in these robberies?" I asked wondering why he provided that information.

"It look's that way. I don't know if these robberies have anything to do with your current investigation, but I found it interesting that you had Joe and Andy's names on your list," Ben replied. "I am currently inputting these names into my deep dive data base and will more interesting information for you tomorrow morning."

"Okay, I'm not going to do anything before I hear back from you tomorrow. You may also brief Sidney on what you have discovered. He may think it is important as I do," I told him as I switched off my phone.

I stood up off the bed, walked over to the window that provided me a view of the almost empty main street of Red Cliff and thought. Maybe, I should talk with Sam Wilcox and see if he knows anything about the robberies that were occurring in Eagle County. I thought the Sheriff wasn't too bright doing this in his own county except he could certainly reduce the chance of apprehending the robbers and keep his plan for a better life intact.

I drove up to the Wise's house and knocked on the door. When Sam answered, I asked, Have you had dinner yet?"

He looked at me with a surprised look on his face and said, "No, I was just getting ready to go down and get me a hamburger tonight. Why?"

"Well, I am going into Minturn tonight to get something besides a hamburger and I thought you might go along to keep me company. While I am there, I want to see if I can find Andy's old red pickup sitting at some bar. I could use another pair of eyes." I explained.

"That's sound good to me. Let me change my clothes and I will join you," he replied as the went into his bedroom.

As he changed his clothes, I went sat down on the couch and relaxed. I thought about when I arrested Sam, the Sheriff asked me in a strong voice if I had the right man. I wondered, if Sam may be part of the robbery ring since the Sheriff knew Sam wasn't the person who killed Ben and Wilma. He knew the prints Officer Jackson took off the body was not Sam's. I decided I needed to be careful until I knew Sam was not involved in the robbery scheme with the Sheriff. I wondered if he would even identify Andy's pickup if he saw it.

On the way to Minturn, I kept thinking about my previous thoughts. I needed to be careful since I really didn't know if Sam was involved or not with the robberies. It seemed to me the Sheriff had recruited some strange people to pull off all these robberies and Sam could be involved after all.

When we arrived, in Minturn it was just six o'clock. "Do you know a good place to eat Sam," I asked.

"There are several different places to eat in Minturn. Most are either Mexican or pizza joints and then a couple only serve breakfast and lunch. There are two that serve what I call American food. One is very small, and we will have to wait to get a table and the other serves great meals but is a little expensive."

"Let's try the expensive one," I said. "Do they have good steaks?"

"I don't know," Sam said. "I could never afford to eat there. I have a friend that said their rib eye steak is to kill for, but it costs Thirty-five-dollars."

"Okay, let the State of Colorado treat you to a good steak tonight," I said as he guided me to the restaurant. It sat on the Eagle River with a balcony that extended out toward the water. The inside was well appointed with some nice art works on the walls. When the receptionist took us to our table, she asked, "Would you like to try one of our famous

The Ghost of Gilman

Bloody Mary's while you decide what you want to order."

"What makes them famous," I asked thinking it was nothing more than a slogan.

She produced a certificate that showed their Bloody Mary's were judge as the best in the West by Time Magazine. "Okay, you convinced me," I said. "Would you like one too Sam?"

He looked at me and said, "Yes, If the State of Colorado is paying for it, I will have one."

We both decided to order the Rib Eye Steak and was very surprised with all of the different items that came with it. The steak was thick, juicy, and cooked just the way we ordered it.

When we finished our waitress presented me with the check. I expected the bill would be about eighty-five-dollars, but the bill came to one-hundred and five dollars. The famous Bloody Mary's cost twenty-dollars apiece.

I looked at Sam and said, "I am happy the State of Colorado is paying this bill."

Sam just smiled, nodded, and said, "I told you it was expensive."

Chapter 9

We got back into the Yukon and drove around the town looking for the red pickup at bars, on and off of the Main Street. As we drove up an alley, I noticed an old red pickup parked on the side of the alley. I pulled the Yukon into a parking place and up to a tall pine tree. I told Sam to wait for me since I had met Andy before and knew what he looked like. I walked around the building and when I walked into the front door. The bar was full of men and a few women. Smoke filled the alcohol tainted air inside. I slowly looked down the bar and at the far end, Andy stood leaning on the bar. He was by himself drinking a beer. He looked up at me and ran out the back door. I ran after him, but one big guy stepped back into my path and almost knock me down. I recovered quickly and as I ran out the back door, I saw the red pickup turning onto Main Street heading toward I-70. I ran to the Yukon and jumped in. Sam said, "He surprised me or else I could have jumped him when he came out. He really tore out of here."

I finally turned onto Main Street and started driving toward I-70. By I came to the entrance and exit roads, there was no site of him in either direction. I looked at Sam and said, "Well at least he knows I want to talk with him. Which way do you think he would go?"

"He could have gone in either direction and I also know that old red pickup is hopped up. He has a new big engine in it and this Yukon would never be able to catch him. I think you should just to back to Red Cliff."

On the way back, Sam kept telling me how much he enjoyed the steak and the Bloody Mary. I dropped him off at the Wise's house and went back to the hotel. I needed to get some sleep, so I just went to bed.

The next morning, I went down to Jaquan's for breakfast. He asked, "How is your investigation going. Do you have any leads?"

I looked at him thinking, why would ask me that question. I simply replied, "No I have nothing so far, but I will keep trying.

I had just finished my breakfast when a couple of old men came in for their morning coffee. I went over to their long table and sat down. "Do you mind if I join you guys?"

"No, everyone is welcome here," one of them said.

Soon four more came in and the subject of the snow and weather started their conversations. Finally, one of the old men asked me, "Do you have any leads on how Bill and Wilma were murdered?"

I looked up and saw Jaquan bending over the counter he was wiping clean so he could hear my answer. I simply said, "You know, this is a very confusing investigation. I don't have any suspects that I can arrest. I think this may be one of those cases that goes unsolved. I had one of those before. No one could be found who would want them dead."

I glanced up at Jaquan who left the counter smiling. This confused me even more. After a little more conversation about other things that happen at the old mine that I found interesting, I went back to the hotel. When I walked in, I noticed that Alice had tears in her eyes.

I walked up to the counter and asked, "What's the matter Alice?

"Oh, the Sheriff is mad at me for letting you look at my room register. He really cussed me out this morning. Can I have it back now?" she said sobbing.

"Yes, of course. I didn't find anything I was looking for anyway so you can tell the Sheriff that the next time you talk with him. I'm going to go up to the loading facility again this afternoon to look for more clues so if he calls and wants to talk with me, you tell him that," I told her.

"Okay, I will. He said he would get back with me later this morning so I will tell him what you told me,"

I went up to my room and got my backpack and left. I drove up to the Wise's house and knocked on the door. Sam opened the door and said, "Come on in. The Sheriff is on the phone with me right now. Let me see what he wants and then we can talk.

I sat down on the couch and listened as Sam picked the phone back up. "Okay Sheriff, what can I do for you?"

I couldn't hear what the Sheriff was saying but I saw Sam's face turn to a troubled look. He finally said, "I don't understand. I owe it to Bill and Wilma. They gave me a place to live and I think I would like to find out who killed them."

He listened again and then said, "Okay, I don't think I can help you but let me think about it. I will call you back later with my answer."

He hung up the phone and turned to me. "The Sheriff wants me to convince you to go back to Denver and let him solve the murder. He doesn't want me to help you in any way. I don't know why but he was very insistent. What do you think of that?"

I sat on the couch dumfounded. I didn't know who to trust anymore. Was Sam involved with the Sheriff. If he wasn't, why would the Sheriff call him. If he was, I could be in extreme danger.

Finally, I said, "Sam, I don't want you to get into any trouble with the Sheriff so I think you should just stay here, and I will continue my investigation. Is that okay with you?"

"Well, that would make the Sheriff happy," He replied.

I stood, shook his hand, and said, "Thanks for joining me for dinner last night. I will let you know when I have this crime solved."

I left the house and drove up to the top of the hill next to the high green bridge on US-24 and called Ben.

When he answered and heard my voice, he said, "Cal, I was just going to call you. You are working in a nest of robbers and probably killers. The Sheriff is definitely involved with the robberies. I have notified Sidney and he is on his way out there right now to arrest him. Sidney hopes he will identify the other people involved in this robbery ring."

I replied, "Okay, I will wait until I hear from Sidney. I'm sure he will call me on his way here. Meanwhile, what did you discover on

Rod Beach

the other people I gave you?"

"Well first of all, I don't think Leland Harvey or Alice Wilson is involved. Leland is just an old sour individual while Alice is completely infatuated with the Sheriff's attention. They have had a sexual arrangement for many years unknown to the Sheriff's wife and family. However, the Alverez brothers, Jaquan and Andy are definitely part of the gang and probably were involved with most of the robberies. The main culprits, Joe Sample and Andy Alvarez, are the two men identified by the camera in the first robbery when they didn't wear any ski masks. You need to be careful with both of these guys. I think they will do anything the Sheriff wants since they think they are protected by the law in Eagle County."

"Wow! That is very interesting. I even took Sam out to dinner last night and later when I encountered Andy Alverez, he didn't stop him from running away when he could have. I definitely need to be on my toes. I guess I need to talk with Sidney now to see what he suggests.

"I think that is a good idea. I don't think you have anyone out there in Red Cliff who you can trust anymore," Ben said.

I switched off my SAT phone and dialed Sidney's cell phone. When he answered, he said, "Cal, I am presently at the Eisenhower Tunnel. I'm going to lose you now."

His phone went dead and so I switched off my SAT phone. Shortly, my phone rang, and Sidney continued. "I am on my way. Ben briefed me earlier this morning and I left immediately. I am driving at a high rate of speed since the roads are open and dry. I also have a State Patrol car ahead of me so I'm making really good time. I should be in vale in about an hour. Why don't you meet me at the Police Station, and we can see what we need to do next. Where are you right now?"

"I got worried about who I could trust out here, so I'm am sitting near the high bridge just outside Red Cliff. I think the Sheriff is on to me since my investigation is getting very close to him. I will leave right now for Vail and I just hope I don't encounter him on the way. If I do see him or any of the other people, I will just drive like a bat out of hell for Vail. I hope to see you there."

Rod Beach

"Be careful Cal and I will see you in an hour," Sidney said as I started driving back toward Minturn. As I passed the Gate to Gilman, I saw a Deputy Sheriff sitting there. I noticed he was asleep behind his steering wheel, so I continued. I passed through Minturn undetected, so I headed east toward Vail.

When I pulled into the Police Station, Chief Dunny met me at the front door. "Thank goodness you made it. Did you see anyone from the Sheriff's department on the way?"

I explained the sleeping deputy at the Gilman gate but indicated I didn't see any one else that could be involved.

He said, "Sidney explained everything to me this morning on his way here. He was very worried about you so I'm happy to see you. I guess you really stirred up a hornet's nest up in Red Cliff area. Can you brief me on what you know so far."

I gave him a complete briefing on what Officer Jackson had determine and what Ben Hamilton had discovered from his deep dive data base on the people I identified. I finally said, "It looks like Sheriff Jameson is the leader of a rather large number of armed robbers. He get a cut of what they take and has made a number of large deposits into his bank account. As a leader, he isn't too bright. If I was him, I would have used another bank account instead of his normal bank account."

"Well in my experience, these types of people are not the most intelligent people, or they would never get involved in the first place. Now I have to warn you from our information, Andy Alverez, Joe Sample and Sam Wilcox are the primary people who are involved in the actual robberies. I told Sidney these men will not give up without a fight."

"I agree with you knowing them as little as I know. I did tell Sam I was going up to the old loading facility this afternoon so I think that will be where they will try to get rid of me. On the way here, I was thinking how I could use that information. I think if we could get to the loading facility before they arrive, we could set up an ambush and arrest the entire gang at one time. I could call Sam and tell him that I want him to meet me at the loading facility at a certain time this afternoon and I'm sure he will then relay that information on to the Sheriff."

"That is a good idea. Sidney will be here by ten this morning, so we can decide what we need to do. I can arrange some officers to go into the bottom of the mine from the north. It is a three-mile hike but that way we won't give anything away. We can take one of our busses to take everyone to the north trail that follows the railroad tracks and then leave so the Sheriff won't see any sign of police cars. We will have to wait until they come but it would be something that could work."

"I agree with you. There are a number of different places for us to hide until they come up to the loading facility. We can the surround them. Then, they will have no way to escape." I said.

Just then, I saw Sidney through the Chief's window pull into the parking lot. He jumped out of his car and came running into the Police Station and directly into the Chief's Office. When he saw me, he came up and gave me a big hug. "You made it out okay. Great. Now what do you think we should do next?"

I explained the plan the Chief and I had devised, and he agreed it would be good.

Sidney then took charge, "I think we should get your squad together Chief and get this plan going. Cal, I think you should call Sam when we get to the north trail and tell him, you are at the loading facility and found something important that could solve this crime. Tell him to call the Sheriff since the batteries on your SAT phone is almost out of power. Tell him to have the Sheriff meet you there as soon as he can. That will give us enough time to get set up for the capture of the entire gang."

The Chief became excited and said, "Sidney, how many officers should I provide?"

Sidney looked at me and asked, "How many men will the Sheriff have with him Cal?"

"Well besides himself, there is Sam, Andy, Joe, and even maybe Jaquan, so that would make possibly five," I replied.

"Okay, I think with you, me, and Cal, we would probably need an additional eight more men. That would give us double what they have. We need to get them all together and have them drop their weapons," Sidney said. "You need to make sure they have their bullet proof vests as well as their assault rifles. We can place them at the best places after we get there. Why don't you have your men come in here now so we can brief them properly before we leave."

The Chief picked up his phone, dialed a number. Lieutenant Kelly, we have a situation were we need our assault force. Please get seven of your best people and come into my office now."

Within five minutes eight officers came into the Chief's office. Even though it was crowded, the Chief opened the meeting and introduced both Sidney and me. He then told them what our mission is and the timing we had to use. He also told them to dress in their assault gear including their assault rifles and meet him in the back of the station at noon. After telling them that, he turned the briefing over to me and I described the situation and why we needed their assistance. I told them how we would hike into the area from the north. I also said as I looked at the Chief, I think we need to park the bus on the County Road 706 that runs off to the southwest about a mile north of where we hit the north trail. That way we will have a way to get the prisoners back to Vail.

The Chief just replied, "Good idea, Cal. I will have our Transportation Officer drive the bus so he will know how to keep the bus out of sight until we need it."

I looked at my watch and saw it was now eleven o'clock. I think we need to leave in about thirty minutes so we can get into position before the Sheriff and his robbers get there. Can we do that?"

"Yes! Men get busy and meet us at the bus in thirty minutes. Let's get these boys," the Chief ordered.

Chapter 10

The squad of seven seasoned police officers, the Chief, Sidney and I all got onto the bus. I noticed it would usually hold twenty people so we would have enough seats to bring the Sheriff and his men back to Vail. The bus driver was the Transportation Officer and even he had on all of his assault gear. Everyone sat silent as we headed for Minturn. As we drove through town several people on the street stopped when they saw the bus with the Vail Police logo on the side.

As we left Minturn, I called Sam. When he picked up the phone I said, "Sam, I'm at

The Ghost of Gilman

Gilman and I think I have found some evidence that will tell me who killed Bill and Wilma. My SAT phone is almost out of batteries so could you please call Sheriff Jameson and have him meet me at the loading facility and I will take him to the evidence." Before I switched of the phone off, I made several unintelligible sounds like my SAT phone had died.

I turned to Sidney and said, "Was that alright?"

"Yes, it was great. It actually sounded like your phone just quit transmitting. When we approach County Road 107, I walked to the front of the bus. "This is the road I want you to bring the bus back and then drive up over the first ridge. I will call you when we have captured the gang so you can come back to the end of the North Trail and pick all of us up."

The Transportation Officer just gave me the OK sign and I went back to my seat. When we reached the trail down the railroad tracks, he stopped the bus and we all got out. He immediately turned the bus around and headed back toward County Road 107. I lead the way down the tracks toward Gilman.

Rod Beach

After we had gone about two miles through the snow-covered trail, I stopped so the squad could rest. Some sat down on a fallen tree while others just sat down in the snow. After about ten minutes, the Chief signaled everyone to stand up and we continued walking down the trail toward the old mine.

We rounded a curve in the canyon and there before us stood the high processing center surrounded by some smaller buildings. The Chief came up to me and Sidney and said, "Where do you want to start dropping off the men?"

I looked at Sidney who said, the processing center has a tower in it where one officer could climb up into a small platform under a window that looks to the south. He would have a good look at the Sheriff's party as they come up the trail. That would be a good place, but it is about one-hundred yards from his position to where Cal will be. Put one of your best shots there."

"Okay," the Chief said. "Jim you climb up in that tall building to where the south facing window is and position yourself, so you have a good view of that small black building on the south end of all the buildings."

The Ghost of Gilman

With those orders Jim started walking to the processing center. He turned to all his Officers and said, Men keep your radios on silent but on receive only in case I have to get in touch with you. I don't want to hear any squawking radios. Now Cal where should I place the rest of the Officers?"

"They should find a suitable place behind the row of buildings or inside them. Try to find a window or some missing boards so you have a view where I will soon be standing. Two of you should find a place below the old tracks on the west side of the loading facility where you are not visible to the men walking up the trail from the south. You must however be able to see me. I will stand out in the open until you all get into a suitable position. Sidney, you take the Chief down to the old Railroad Station. From the waiting room, you will be able to peer out of the windows on the south side of the waiting room and see the Sheriff and his men coming up the trail. When they get close to where I will meet them, you move closer to the edge of the drop-off from my level to the new Station level. Chief, I want you to take charge of when you will call out to them to drop their weapons and they are under arrest. I think at that time and the confusion that will result, will give me enough time to dive into the loading facility behind the wall. Does everyone understand?"

The Chief said, "Okay men let's do this right. Cal is taking a big chance they want to see the evidence he said he had, so I don't think they will harm him immediately. However, when I make my declaration to drop their weapons, You should make yourselves visible but able to duck behind something if they start firing. Do you understand me. One more thing, Do not, I repeat do not shoot Cal."

I smiled and said, "Thanks Chief. I needed that. Okay let's get into position. If I know the Sheriff, he should be here in about a half an hour or a little longer. Keep aware and we will be successful."

Everyone started getting in position. After a few minutes, I looked to check on the position of everyone and found all but one. I wondered if he was just well hidden or if he couldn't see me. I waited for a minute or two and started waiving ate each of the officers and they each waved back. Then I saw an officer waving back at me that I had not been able to find. He had positioned himself behind a big old ore car and was lying on the ground between the tracks just behind the first set of wheels. These guys are good, I thought. I walked over and looked down at the Train Station thinking Sidney and the Chief had a warmer place to stake out. I saw Sidney peek out of his window and I began to think I may live through this after all.

After standing in front of the loading facility for over thirty minutes, I decided to go inside to get out of the cold wind. I sat down on the old desk and relaxed as much as I could. I still smelled the odor of the two bodies. I thought I saw a rat run across the floor and quickly grabbed for my side arm, but it was a just a small weed that had blown in through the open door to join the other weeds in the corner of the room.

I sat there for what seemed to be over an hour, but when I looked at my watch, I had been in the facility for just a half hour. Suddenly, I heard a loud voice. I peered out the open door and the was the Sheriff framed by the door casing. I walked out to the middle of the wide roadway in front of the buildings and said, "Hi Sheriff, did you come by yourself?"

The Sheriff didn't answer but just let out a loud high-pitched whistle. I looked to the south and Sam Wilcox and Andy Alvarez walking up from the far side of the loading conveyor. Then, Joe Sample stepped out behind me from the open space between the loading facility and the loading augur.

I looked at the Sheriff and asked, "Why did you bring these men along?"

These men are my special deputies and I use them to protect me. Now where is this evidence you found."

Just then I heard the Chief yell, Sheriff, drop your weapons. You are surrounded. Don't be foolish so we would have to shoot you. Drop them now!"

Sam immediately dropped his rifle. Andy looked around and couldn't see anyone to shoot at, so he dropped his as well. But Joe raised his weapon and aimed directly at me.

I heard a shot ring out. I thought he had pulled his trigger? I didn't feel anything and then I saw Joe drop lifeless into the snow.

The Ghost of Gilman

Sheriff Jameson looked at me and then at Chief Dunny who was now standing on the berm next to the Railroad Station and said, "I knew you were good, but not this good."

I pulled out my side arm and said, "Sheriff, if you want to live, I would suggest you drop your rifle and side arm."

He let his rifle fall to the ground and pulled his side arm out of it's holster carefully by only two fingers and let it fall to the earth. Then Sidney came running up to where we all were standing looking at each other and said, "Sheriff have your men get on their knees and you too." Sidney said as the picked up the Sheriff's rifle and side arm.

Chief Dunny came running up to where we were and said, "Ralph Jameson, you are under arrest for the murder of William and Wilma Wise and armed robbery of numerous establishments in Eagle County. Do you understand these charges?"

Jameson looked at Chief Dunny and said, "I have never killed anyone."

The Chief then turned to each of the Sheriff's remaining henchmen and said, "Sam Wilcox and Andy Alverez, you are also under arrest for the murder of William and Wilma Wise and for armed robbery of numerous establishments. Do you understand these charges?"

They both looked at Jameson and said, "Yes, we do."

By this time, all seven of the Vail Police Assault Squad had assembled around the three men who remained standing with their hand cuffed behind their backs.

I walked up to Jameson and said, "We are taking you to the Vail Police Jail and then you will be tried in the Fifth District Court in Glenwood Springs. How do you plead?

"I plead not guilty," He replied.

I told the same thing to each of the other two men and they both followed the Sheriff's choice of not guilty.

I had an Assault Officer take each prisoner to a different location so they could not generate a single story to tell the judge and sat them down. I turned to Chief Dunny and said, "Chief, we have one dead culprit. We need to make a stretcher to carry his body out of here. I will get some metal roofing material and Sidney and I will build a sled that we can use to drag him back to the bus. Can I get a couple of your men to help me?"

"Of course. Henry and Alan, you go with Detective York to bring some metal sheets back here."

They followed me and I walked behind the processing facility where the roof had fallen into the main structure, I had the two officers each pull one eight-foot long sheet off the roof. When I returned, I saw two officers sitting on the ground on each side of Jameson and two others were sitting with Sam and two more with Andy. The Chief had all three prisoners separated from each other by at least fifty yards.

By the time I laid the two metal roofing sheets down on the ground, Sidney had again found some wire. He used the same long nail and punched a hole in each sheet and put the wire through it on one end and twisted it tight. He then unrolled the roll of wire and formed a handle about six feet from the front edge of the metal sheets. The two officers then picked up Joe Sample and laid him onto the makeshift sled.

Once we had everything in order, Chief had

the biggest man start pulling the sled over the snow toward where we were going to meet the bus. He then had the two officers who were holding Jameson walk along on both sides with one hand on his arm and the other hand on his cuffed hand. Then, he had the officer who was sitting with Andy Alverez stand him up and said, "Sidney, will you join Officer Percell in marching his guy back to the bus. Cal you and Officer Pruitt take Sam Wilcox. Make sure there is enough space so they can not communicate with each other. I will follow everyone and when we get close, I will call our Transportation Officer to come and pick us up."

The entire troop walked like we had rehearsed it many times before. The caravan walked slowly back north along the railroad tracks. When we rounded the last curve in the trail, I saw the bus there waiting for us.

The drill was the same as before. I sat with Officer Pruitt and had Sam Wilcox between us in the back seat of the bus, Sidney sat with Officer Percell with Andy Alverez between them, and the two officers who had Jameson by the arms sat in the front seat. Chief Dunny opened the back door of the bus and slide the dead body of Joe Sample into the space normally used for luggage. He then climbed in and stood facing the entire squad as the Transportation Officer started driving back to Vail.

He drove up to their new jail and one by one, the Chief removed each prisoner and placed them each into a sound proof jail cell. When he had completed that transfer, he thanked his squad and said, "That is why we train all the time. You officers should be proud of how this episode went down. That was a very good job guys."

He turned to Sidney and I and said, "I would like a cup of hot coffee. How about you?"

We went into his office and sat down with a cup of coffee and reviewed our capture process.

I asked, "You taught me some new techniques today Chief. Where did you learn how to keep those crooks separated?"

I took a six-month course at the FBI School in Quantico, Virginia. They showed us how to handle these kinds of arrests. It think it all worked out very well don't you?"

Rod Beach

I looked at Sidney and said, "Yes I did. It worked out basically as we planned it. I was surprised that we had to kill Joe Sample, but I understand he was a hard case anyway?"

"Yes, we have had our eye on him for some time. Now I have to make a report to the Eagle County Board of Commissioners so they can start the process of getting a new Sheriff. What are you going to do?"

"Well, I think Sidney and I should pay a visit to Jaquan Alverez to determine how much he was involved in the Sheriff's operation. Then I need to inform Bill and Wilma's children what has happen and where they can pick up their parents. They are still in your morgue, aren't they?

"Yes, and they can stay there until they make arrangements to have them taken to an undertaker. Do you know where they would want to bury them?"

"I have no idea, but I will find out," I said. "I think we will go back to Red Cliff and lock up their house and talk with Jaquan to see if he is involved. If he is, we will bring him back here so he can be tried with the others."

Chief Dunny looked at Sidney and asked,

The Ghost of Gilman

"Do you want to talk with each of our criminals?

Sidney looked at me and said, "Yes, we need to get their statements so we can start working up our court case. I would like to interview each of them in a room where we can record their statements. Do you have and interrogation room with that capability?"

"Yes, I had one built just for this type of interrogation. Who do you want to talk with first?" the Chief asked.

Sidney looked at me and I said, I would like to talk with Sam Wilcox first. I have become acquainted with him. In fact, we had dinner together just last night in Minturn. I think he would be able to give us more information than the others, so bring him into the interrogation room and Sidney and I will start questioning him."

The Chief picked up his phone and told someone to bring Sam Wilcox into the interrogation room.

Sidney and I had just sat down and had opened our notebooks when the door opened, and a guard brought Sam in. I motioned him to set on the opposite side of the table and we began.

"I looked at Sam and said, "I was very surprised to see you with the Sheriff Sam. How did you get involved with him?

Sam looked around the room and didn't see any tape recorders or cameras, so he began. I was out of work and had just moved into Bill and Wilma's house when we started talking about all of the robberies that were occurring on I-70. Bill told me he was filling up his old car in Minturn, when he saw Andy and Joe leave the Filling Station and Convenience Store in Minturn. Bill told me both of them were taking off a ski mask as they got into a car and sped away toward I-70. I thought that was unusual and when I saw Andy a couple of days later, I told him what Bill had seen. He became excited and said, I should come with him. He took me down to Eagle and into the Sheriff's office.

 When I told the Sheriff what Bill had told me, he looked at Andy and said, we need to take care of them. Then he asked me what I did for a living. I told him I was currently unemployed, but I normally worked in timber business and I was now living with

The Ghost of Gilman

Bill and Wilma."

"Did he ask you to join his band of robbers then?" I asked.

"No, he said I should go back to their place and see how much more they saw? I did, and that night I asked Bill again if he was sure it was Andy and Joe who had robbed the place."

Sidney asked quickly, "Did Bill elaborate on the descriptions of the two men?"

"Yes, he said he knew both of them well and was thinking of going into the Sheriff's office and tell him what he saw. I went down to Jaquan's and saw Andy talking with his brother, so I told him about what Bill saw. That was when Andy took me back to the Sheriff and he asked me to help him silence Bill."

"Did you agree to help him?" I asked.

"Not at first but he said if I did, he would pay me five-hundred dollars. I needed the money, so I agreed. I didn't know that he was going to kill both of them. You have to believe me. I really liked both of them."

"What happen next?" I asked.

Rod Beach

The next day the Sheriff was in Red Cliff and he asked me to come to his room and talk. When I arrived, he outlined his plan. He said he wanted to scare Bill and Wilma to keep then from talking. He told me to take them up to Gilman and he would be waiting for them and try to convince them they had made a mistake with their thoughts that Andy and Joe robbed the store and gas station. I talked with Bill and said, I would like to go see the old Gilman town so Bill, Wilma and I all went up to the town. When we were just leaving the old Community Center a shot rang out almost hitting Bill. I ducked behind a wall and then I saw Bill and Wilma running toward the south of the row of big houses. A short time later, Andy and Joe showed up and asked me where they went. I pointed in the direction and they said follow us and they took off after the two old people. As we came to the edge of the canyon, they saw a little used narrow trail leading to the bottom of the canyon. We followed them quickly and when we reached the place where the land slide was, we saw them sliding down and were almost to the bottom. All three of us jump and slide down behind them and started looking in the building in the bottom of the canyon. When we entered the old loading facility, Bill was sitting at his old desk and Wilma was standing behind him."

"Did the Sheriff kill him there?" I asked.

"No not immediately. He talked with Bill and Wilma trying to get them to keep quiet about the robbery, but Bill said, he couldn't since his son was a lawyer and he was going to call him to see what he suggest he does. That made the Sheriff mad, so he asked Joe, do you have that ice pick you always carry? Joe reached into the inside pocket of his coat and pulled out a long thin ice pick. He had me and Andy hold Bill and Wilma's arms behind their back and Joe stuck that ice pick into each of their chests. They each yelled in pain and slowly passed out. The Sheriff told Joe and Andy to just lay them down on the floor beside each other and we left. Since we didn't know how to get back up to the Sheriff's car, we walked down to Red Cliff. Then Andy drove the Sheriff and Joe back to the Sheriff's car and I walked home thinking about what had just happened. It then started to snow, and it kept snowing all the rest of that day and all night. The next time

Rod Beach

I saw Andy at his brother's bar I asked him if he would take me up to the Gilman the next morning to get Bill's car. He agreed and I went up there as soon as the road was cleared and drove it back down to Red Cliff. I decided to leave Red Cliff, so I took what I needed and put the other stuff in Bill and Wilma's bedroom, so my room looked to be empty. I started driving toward Minturn and then realized, you probably had put out an APB for the car. After thinking about what had just happened, I turned around and returned to the house. That is when you found me Cal."

"Okay Sam, you became a witness to a murder. You also were threatened by both Andy and Joe as well as the Sheriff. Will you testify in court about what happened?"

Sam hesitated, "I guess I can. I never was in on any of the robberies and was duped into the murder. I became ashamed that I was there holding Wilma's arms when Joe thrust that long ice pick into her heart. I almost fainted at that time. I have never done anything like this before."

Sidney looked at me and said, "I think we probably have all of the ring in jail but there may be someone above the Sheriff who was calling the shots for the robbery ring. I think I will take Sam with me back to Denver and put him into protective custody until the trial. I'm afraid, he knows too much to be out here in the wild west. Is that alright with you Sam?"

"Yes, I will be happy to testify in court and will accept my punishment. I will go with you since I'm sure I am not safe here since I do know too much and was basically an uninformed bystander in the entire episode," Sam Said.

Sidney stood and immediately the Officer outside that was recording and videotaping the entire confession, came into the interrogation room. He escorted him back to his cell and said, "Chief Kingsbury, we will hold him in his cell until you are ready to leave Vail."

As they left, Sidney said, "Well that was an interesting story. We need to try to collaborate it when we interrogate Andy Alverez and Sheriff Jameson. Lets talk with Andy next.

Within minutes, an officer brought Andy Alverez into the room. We motioned him to sit and the officer forced him down into a chair. Sidney began, "Andy, you know why we want to talk with you. You are going to be charged with murder and robbery. You can help yourself if you decide to tell us what happened that day in Gilman."

Andy looked around the room and then said, "I don't know nutten about any murder. Yes, I will admit to robbing some places since I know you have video of one, but I didn't kill anyone."

I stood over him looking down with a strong look and said, "We know you killed William and Wilma Wise. We know you used an ice pick to puncture their hearts and let them slowly bleed to death. You might as well tell us what happened since you are going to be convicted and probably sentenced to death for these murders."

The look on Andy's face turn from one of strength to one of doubt. "It was the Sheriff's idea since old man Wise had seen me and Joe leave one of our robberies. The Sheriff said we needed to make it look like they died naturally so Joe suggested using a long ice pick to stick in their heart. We knew after he did that, they would never be able to make it back to Red Cliff alive. I never did anything but hold the old man's arms behind his back while Joe stuck each of them. The Sheriff should go to jail as well since he was the one who made us do that. I did not want to kill anyone. That's all I'm going to say until my day in court and then I will spill the beans on the Sheriff and his boss."

Sidney looked at me and winked. Sure enough, the Sheriff had someone else connected with all of the robberies.

"Well, if you are going to jail for robbery and as an accomplish to murder, you will spend probably over thirty or forty years in jail. How old will you be by the time you get out?" I asked.

"I told you I'm not going to name names. I don't want to be killed in prison either. All I can say, look for the richest person in Red Cliff and you will find the brains to this whole operation and who actually ordered the murder of those two old people. I can also tell you, it was Joe Sample who plunged a long ice pick into each of their hearts, so he is the actual killer and you took care of him at Gilman. So, I will be happy to go and take my sentence for robbery and then I should be out in less than ten years. I have already called my lawyer and he said to only tell you what I have told you."

Sidney smiled and said, "Thanks for the information Andy." Then turning to me he said, "I guess we need to go to Red Cliff and arrest Jaquan for murder."

Andy jumped up and said, "Are you telling me you think it was my brother. You guys are dumber than I thought. The richest person in Red Cliff is the woman who runs the hotel. She not only charges an outlandish price for a room, she takes thirty percent of everything we get from the robberies. Over the years, she probably had netted over one-hundred-thousand dollars."

Sidney smiled and winked at me and then said, "Well Andy, since you lawyer advised you not to talk to us or tell us anything, I guess we should just let you return to you jail cell."

The officer outside immediately came into the room and escorted Andy out. Sidney looked at me and exclaimed, "I guess he just wanted to follow the advice of his council.

The Ghost of Gilman

He is not too bright since he told us what we needed to determine. I think just to make sure we have talked with everyone, let's spend some time with Jameson.

Soon the door of the room opened and there stood Jameson in both hand and legs chains. I motioned him to sit and he did. I looked at him and shook my head. "Sheriff, how did you get mixed up in all of this? Why did you have to kill those two old people anyway?"

Jameson just smiled and said, "I have nothing to say until my trial."

"Well, at least you can tell us about how you ran the robbery ring?" Sidney said.

"I again say, I will not tell you anything until my trial," he reiterated.

"Okay," I said, "You should know your underlings have told us exactly how your organization operated including the death of William and Wilma Wise and have listed you as the main director of everything. Your lawyer should know that. If he understands the situation you are in and what we already know he may advise you to respond differently. Now, will you tell us what we want to know?"

"This is not my first interrogation. I know how to interrogate people as well as you two. I respectfully request that I cannot and will not provide any information concerning why I was arrested," he repeated looking directly at me. "I will probably see you again in court and then you will hear my story and why I am not responsible for all of these charges against me."

"Okay, I guess we are through here Cal," Sidney said as he looked hard at the former Sheriff. "Let's get him back behind bars. We will certainly see you in court."

The Ghost of Gilman

Chapter Eleven

As we left the interrogation room, Sidney suggested we talk with Chief Dunny again and let him know what we have discovered. He said he would process each of the prisoners and then contact the County Attorney.

Sidney suggested, "I think you should first check with the State Attorney General Gary Olsen, since he may want to try them in State Court since it is both a murder as well as a robbery case and that the CBI was involved in solving the crime."

"Okay, that would probably be better since it

does involve a County Sheriff. I will let you know Sidney, what the State Attorney General Says. Thanks for both of your help. What are you and Cal going to do now?"

I replied before Sidney could and said, "I want to go back and close up the Wise's house and take the key to their daughter in Denver. Their son and her may want to come out and get some personal items to keep. I also wonder if there may also be another one or two people involved so I still want to talk with them just to satisfy my curiosity. Then we will probably go back to Denver tonight."

Sidney nodded his head and said, "I have learned from Cal that he always has some other ideas on most of his cases, so I'm going with him to make sure everything is complete."

We left the Vail Police Station and drove over to Red Cliff. We stopped by Jaquan's place but found a young girl tending bar and handling the three guests in the place. "Do you know where Jaquan is?" I asked.

"Yes, he is over at the Mountain View Hotel. You can find him there."

Rod Beach

We drove up to the hotel and walked in and was surprised to see Jaquan behind the counter. "What are you doing here" I asked.

"I own this place now. Alice left this afternoon and said she was leaving Red Cliff, so I bought the place from her."

"Wow! That's news. Do you know why she left?" I inquired.

"No, she just said she needed a change of scenery. I got a great deal. She sold me this place for my Mercedes." He responded.

"What?" Sidney exclaimed. "You did get a great deal. How long ago did she leave?"

He looked at his watch and said, "I guess it was about two hours ago. She just threw some clothes into the back seat, took all the cash out of her wall safe, and left. She didn't say where she was headed."

"What color of Mercedes was your car?" I asked.

"It was a coal black 2010 Mercedes sedan, he responded.

Sidney took out his SAT phone and started dialing a number. He stopped and asked

The Ghost of Gilman

Jaquan, "What was the license plate number"

"I didn't have a number. My plates just read 'Red Cliff'.

Sidney finished dialing a familiar number and when someone answered, he said, "This is Sidney Kingsbury of the CBI. I want to put out an APB for a 2010 black Mercedes with the words 'Red Cliff' on the license plate. The person driving is wanted and is probably driving either east or west on I-70. If you stop this person, let me know at this number immediately and then take her to the Vail Police Department for questioning. Tell the police in Vail, I will be there soon to question her."

All this time Jaquan stood looking at us with a puzzled look on his face. "What is going on?" he finally asked.

We explained what had happened earlier today and that his brother was involved. He listen shaking his head as we told the entire story. Finally, Sidney asked, "Are you involved in this robbery scheme?"

"No, I am not. I often wondered how Andy Got his money and now I know. Andy was always a rebel and always was getting in trouble. I tried to get him to help me at the bar, but he didn't want to work. I thought now that I purchased this place, he could take over the bar but if he is guilty of robbery and possible murder, I can forget about that," he explained.

We both believed him since he was talking very sincere with a lot of remorse. "Well," I said, "We need to go up and close up the Wise house. We are locking it up for their children. They may want some of the personal items there so we will take the key to them.

We made sure there was enough fuel oil in the tank that ran their furnace and turned it down to sixty degrees just to keep the pipes from freezing. I closed the door and locked it putting the keys into my pocket.

Sidney looked at me with a question, "Are you ready now to start home?"

"Yes, however I want to question Alice. I wonder why she thought she needed to leave in such a hurry especially since she sold the

hotel at such a low price. I think she may be

involved with the others who are in the jail in Vail."

"I had the same thought," Sidney said. "Maybe we can get lucky and the State Patrol will catch her by the time we get back to Vail."

We had just passed through Minturn when my cell phone rang. I handed it to Sidney to answerer since I was driving. He answered the call and said, "This is Sidney Kingsbury. How can I help you?"

After listening for a few seconds, Sidney said that's great. Cal and I will be their in about fifteen minutes. Make sure she doesn't talk to any of the other prisoners. We have some questions to ask her."

He listened again and simply said "Okay," before switching off the phone.

"The Chief has her in his office and will keep her there until we arrive. He said she is really mad and is yelling at everyone who is around her," Sidney related.

"Well, let's see what she has to say when we talk with her," I said as I started formulating a plan of interrogation.

When we pulled up in front of the Police Station, we jumped out and walked into the Chief's office. Alice as sitting handcuffed in a chair facing the Chief just yelling at him with vial language.

When she saw me, she turned her yelling at me. I held up my hand and said, "Settle down Alice. We have arrested Andy Alverez and Sam Wilcox and shot Joe Sample when he tried to kill us during the arrest. During interrogation they all told us all about you and the Sheriff."

"Those dirty bastards. After all that I have done to make their life better with all the money, they now have turned on me. What a bunch of bastards."

"That is the way it happens sometimes," I said. "Now, why don't you make it easier on yourself and admit to being the leader of this band of thieves. The one thing they didn't say is how you convinced the Sheriff to join your bandits."

"Well, in the beginning, he started coming in to the hotel just to visit me. He kept telling me how his wife didn't love him anymore so one night I took him upstairs and we made love. After that, he would visit me every week. I had also convinced Joe and Andy to start robbing the different stores along I-70. Everything was going well until Jameson started to get too close to solving the robberies. The next time he came, I took him back upstairs and after we made love, I convinced him to start organizing the robberies for a cut of the take. At first, he was not too keen on that idea, but he changed his mind when I threatened him that I would tell his wife about us. He then became an active member of our gang. I was able to get more money than I ever had before. He also enjoyed the extra money and even took that ugly wife of his on a trip to Los Angeles for a week.

"Why did you want Bill and Wilma dead. Why was that?" I asked her.

"One day, Wilma was walking home just as Jameson left the hotel and he turned and kissed me goodbye. Wilma saw it and then after church, she asked me what was going on," Alice explained. "I thought Wilma was a bright woman would sooner or later figure out what was going on. I had left my purse at the church and Wilma found it. I had over a thousand dollars in it and Wilma asked how I ever got that much money. Then Sam Wilcox, who I convinced to join my gang, over heard Wilma talking on the phone to her daughter about me and all money I had. I guess I should have just let it go, but I couldn't. I called Jameson to come down and after we had a long night together, I convinced him that Wilma probably also told Bill so the Sheriff came up with a plan that would look like they just died while visiting the old Ghost town. Sam asked them to take him to Gilman on that day and they did. You probably know the rest by now. You have to find Jameson. He was the one who killed that old couple."

"Yes, but Alice Wilson, you are the responsible person for all of the robberies and the death of William and Wilma Wise. You are now under arrest for not only robbery but murder as well. Chief, place her into a separate cell away from the others and if you want, we will transport them later in the week to Denver for trial."

"Cal, that was an extraordinary confession.

The Ghost of Gilman

I have everything she said on tape. You will have verbal proof of what she said. I look forward to spending a few days in Denver during their trials. I have already called the State Attorney General and he recommends they stand trial in State Court, so he is sending the vans to take each of them down to Denver. I want to thank you again for such a professional job," the Chief said. "I guess you and Sidney can go on home since everything at this end will be handled by the State of Colorado."

Since I had my Yukon and Sidney had his car, we each got into our vehicles and headed for Denver. We stopped in Georgetown since it was now about seven o'clock and had a bite to eat. While we sat after our meal drinking another cup of coffee, I called Joan Ault and filled her in on everything that had happened. I told her I had the keys to her parent's house and if she wanted them, she could stop by tomorrow and pick them up at my office.

"When will the trial be?" She asked.

"We don't know right now but they will be tried in State Court. I will keep you informed on when it will occur," I replied.

"I think both Al and I want to be there during the different trials so please keep us informed," she said as she hung up her phone.

As we got back into the car and headed toward Denver, I asked Sidney, "Do you think all of the gang will be charged with murder like I told them?"

"Yes, your charge was a correct charge. Most Judges separates murder into two degrees, that is, first and second-degree murder. This also includes voluntary and involuntary manslaughter as separate crimes that do not constitute murder. As you know, first-degree murder is any murder that is willfully conducted and premeditated with malice aforethought. In this case, I believe the Judge will use the Joint Enterprise Laws as the basis for his judgement," Sidney related some information that I didn't understand.

"What is the Joint Enterprise Law? I asked Sidney.

He smiled and replied, "The simplest form of joint enterprise to murder is when two or more people make plans to cause death and doing so if all the parties participated in carrying out the plan, all are liable. This is true regardless of who actually inflicted the fatal injury. However, when there is no plan to murder and one party kills while carrying out a plan to do something else, such as a planned robbery in which the participants hope to be able to get what they want without killing anyone, but one of them in fact kills, the other participants may still be guilty of murder or manslaughter if they had the necessary means to stop the murder. I expect that all of the Sherriff's men will have to stand up to a murder charge since this is the case with this murder.

"I guess, I feel sorry for Sam Wilcox since he may not have known the gang was going to kill the two old people. I think he should only be up for manslaughter instead of murder.

"Well that will be up to the Judge. Do you know if he ever tried to keep the gang from killing Ben and Wilma?" Sidney inquired.

"No, he never told me that. In fact, he was carrying a weapon so he must have known they were going to kill the two old people. I guess you are right," I said thinking about what Sidney had said. "I guess I should trust the State Attorney General to make the right charge."

Rod Beach

When we entered the CBI Office, the receptionist saw us and said, "Chief Kingsbury, the Attorney General is in your office and is waiting for you."

We both went into Sidney's office and saw Kenneth Norman, the Attorney General sitting in one of Sidney's side chair reading some notes. He stood when we entered and shook our hands.

"You guys have really been busy. Chief Dunny of Vail said that you have arrested another person in the Wise murders. He said you were on your way home, so I just came over to hear about your latest arrest."

Sidney looked at me and I started to explain what I knew and why I arrested Alice James. After telling the entire story of my investigation to Kenneth Norman, I asked, "Have you received the fingerprint information from the National Data base yet?"

"Yes, Officer Jackson forwarded them to me this afternoon. The prints on the body are Joe Sample's and Andy Alverez's. Your Officer Jackson also sent me his entire book on what he found during his autopsy. He is very competent."

The Ghost of Gilman

After I finished with my complete investigation, he sat back and said, "You did an outstanding job Detective York. I think we will have an excellent case for a Joint Enterprise Case. This will be my first experience with a case like this. You will be my expert witness and I think we can put this gang away for a number of years. I am also putting a hold on all of their bank accounts in an effort to get some of the money back to the people they robbed."

I reached into my brief case and pulled out a stack of money that I took from Alice when we booked her.

He counted the money and said, "You did give her a receipt for this money, didn't you?"

"Yes, and the receipt was signed by Chief Dunny as well as me. We counted it out in front of her and asked her where she got it and she just replied she had saved it. Chief Dunny made a copy of the receipt as well."

"That's good," he said. "I need to take this money so we can use it during the trial. I will also give you a receipt for the money," He said as he opened up his brief case and took out a receipt and signed it.

Rod Beach

I looked at Attorney Wilson and asked, "You said you were going to try this gang using the Joint Evidence Case. What does that mean?"

"It is basically a legal term that is used in murder cases where a number of people in a gang are present during the murder. The Judge can rule under the Joint Evidence that all members of the gang is guilty of murder even though only one of the gang actually did the murder. The other members are liable since they did not try to stop the murder, so they jointly are guilty of murder. In this case the Sheriff's gang, including the leader, Alice James, are therefore guilty of murder and can be sentence as such," he replied.

"Wow, that is something I have never heard of before," I said.

"Yes, it is relatively new and was developed for the trial of gang members. It is designed to get these gang members off the streets effectively," he replied.

Sidney asked, "When do you think the trial will be?"

"I expect the Judge will set it up rather

quickly since the newspapers have all had feature stories today on the capture of this gang. You probably do not have to prepare too much since what you have told me, is what I will have you tell the jury. They need to understand how hard this investigation was and how complicated it became with all of the members of the gang arrested, Norman said trying to educate both of us on this new law. "When someone is charged in criminal court with a gang allegation for participating in a crime, the criminal prosecutors will have to prove that:

1. The person or persons has actively participated in a criminal gang activity,
2. When person who participated in the criminal gang, he or she knew that the gang engages in a pattern of criminal activity,
3. The person willfully assisted the criminal conduct by the members of the criminal gang by one of the following: directly committing a criminal felony act himself or aiding and abetting another member of the criminal gang to commit a criminal felony.

"Well that shouldn't be a problem," I replied.

Rod Beach

Norman looked at me and said, "I will not have to prove that a person accused of participation in a criminal gang was an actual member of the gang or that the person devoted a substantial amount of time to the criminal gang. It is enough that the person has some role to make an allegation against that person."

"Does that apply to someone like Sam Wilcox who didn't know the Sheriff was going to kill Bill and Wilma? I asked.

"Yes, I won't have to prove every person involved in the actual criminal activity when it took place. When a person is charged with a crime and has a gang allegation, the jury may use the crime charged to determine if in fact gang activity was involved. I will have to show the jury that there was a pattern of criminal gang activity. I also have to show the jury two or more crimes does satisfy the requirements discussed above were committed. That should not be a problem in this case since the gang did rob a number of different establishments," he said smiling.

"What kind of penalty will the gang members get?" I asked.

The Ghost of Gilman

Norman looked at me and said, "That will be up to the Judge. However, the law is pretty definitive. Participation in a criminal gang is a crime itself. The Judge has can charged them with either a felony or a misdemeanor. A person who is convicted of participating in a criminal gang may be sentenced to imprisonment in the county jail for a period not to exceed one year if it is a misdemeanor and by imprisonment in the state prison for sixteen months, or two or three years if the conviction is for a felony crime. Additionally, any person who participates in a criminal gang with knowledge of its nature, and who willfully promotes, assists, or benefits from any of the criminal activity of the members of the gang may be charged with conspiracy to commit the felony charged against other members as a coconspirator. This is a much lesser level of involvement than what is required without the criminal gang allegation and often time people who had only a minor role in a crime can be charged as if they were the actual perpetrators."

"Well, I know Sam did not participate in any of the robberies and was simply paid $500 to take the gang up to the mine that day. I don't believe he knew they were going to kill the Wise's." I said thinking that Sam should not be charged with the same crimes as the other members of the gang.

"The problem for most people is not the actual charge, but the enhancements that apply if a crime is charged and a criminal street gang enhancement is also alleged. Often times the penalties associated with that enhancement will be much greater than the actual charge. In fact, this is the case more often than not," Norman responded. "If a person is convicted of any felony crime where the penalty is less than life in prison that is committed for the benefit of, at the direction of, or in association with a criminal street gang, the criminal court will add an additional two, three, or four years to the sentence at the criminal court's discretion. If, however the felony is defined as serious felony by the Penal Code, the court will add five years to the original sentence. If the felony is defined as a violent felony by the Penal Code, then the court will add 10 years to any sentence. For example if a person is found guilty of the crime of assault with a deadly weapon, the court may sentence them to either 3, 5 or 7 years but then add another ten years simply because the gang allegation was sustained."

"Well, I believe that Sam was an unknowing participant in the crime. He actually helped me solve this crime by telling me about the robberies and the relationship they had with the Sheriff," I explained.

"In that case, a person can also be charged as a conspirator despite having a minimal involvement in the crime. That means that the person may be charged with any additional non-gang enhancements as if he were the actual perpetrator. This can add several years to the person's sentence as well. For example, if a firearm was discharged during the crime an additional 20 years will be added to the sentence not just to the person who shot it, as would have been the case without a gang allegation, but to everyone present because of the gang allegation," he replied.

"Well, I want to testify that Sam did not know the Sheriff was going to kill William and Wilma Wise. I will also testify that he assisted me in identifying all of the participants except for the Ring Leader Alice

James. Would the Judge then make an exception in his case?" I stated strongly.

"Yes, he most likely would. However, he will still probably be sentenced to at least one year in the State Prison. The gangs have become so strong that the legislature has created these laws to protect the people of Colorado."

With that, he stood, shook both of our hands and left Sidney's office.

Sidney looked at me and said, "Why don't you take a couple of days off. I know you don't agree with the State's Attorney, but the law is the law. You need to forget about this case and when the trial is set, you just let the court decide the fate of all the gang. I think you deserve some time at home with your family after this case. You might be able to even warm up a little. I know I'm going home to my wife and climb in bed so she can warm me up as well. I'll see you in a couple of days."

When I went back to my office to gathered up my things my phone started ringing. When I answered it, Joan Ault started speaking. "I just thought you should know that Al and I have decided to bury mom and dad in

The Ghost of Gilman

Gilman. He always said there were so many ghosts there so we thought two more would be good. Can you get us permission to bury them there?"

"I think I can arrange that Joan and I also think your mother and father, who spent most of their life there would agree with your decision. When do you want the funeral to be?

"We told the Chief of Police at Vail, we would take them to the mortuary there and then right out to the old cemetery in Gilman. He said we could probably do it next week, She replied sadly.

"Okay, I will have the new Eagle County Sheriff escort you into the cemetery so they can be laid to rest forever. I'm sorry for your loss but I think your parents will rest in peace in their home in Gilman."

Rod Beach

The Ghost of Gilman

Rod Beach

Made in the USA
Las Vegas, NV
19 October 2023